THE HAUNTING OF TABITHA GREY

Vanessa Curtis

EGMONT

EGMONT

We bring stories to life

The Haunting of Tabitha Grey first published in
Great Britain 2012
by Egmont UK Limited
239 Kensington High Street
London W8 6SA

ISBN 978 1 4052 5721 3

1 3 5 7 9 10 8 6 4 2

A CIP catalogue record for this title is available from
the British Library

Typeset by Avon DataSet Ltd, Bidford on Avon, Warwickshire
Printed and bound in Great Britain by the CPI Group

Whilst this book is based on real

To Dad, for giving me
a love of ghost stories

Prologue

When Dad first crunches the car up the semi-circular gravel drive outside Weston Manor I don't take much notice.

My head's tipped forwards on the seat and Mum's got a wad of tissues stuffed up my nostril and is telling me to keep still. Ben is crying next to me, impatient to get out of the car where he's been sitting stuck next to a pile of cases and boxes for a hot half-hour.

Nosebleeds.

I hate them.

Gran says that they're a sign of a 'sensitive soul' and that all the best people get nosebleeds at my age. But that's not much comfort when you're swallowing salty blood that runs down the back of your throat and your mother is yelling at you not to move and your father is drumming his fingers on the car window with impatience, is it?

Nope.

Gran's not moving in with us, anyway. There was some talk of it, cos she's living on her own now and not very mobile, but Mum and Dad had one of their rare frosty conversations and Dad was heard to utter the words, 'If that lunatic is moving in, I'm moving out,' and since then it hasn't been mentioned again. Besides, she's only half an hour away from here by car.

Dad's switched the engine off now and as the blood finally dries up in my nose I become aware of how quiet it is.

'It's beautiful,' Mum says. She's gazing up at the house in front of us. 'Like a palace!'

I shoot her an astonished look when she says that. Even Ben stops fiddling about and stares at her.

'But it's not,' I say, 'like a palace. This is just a house.'

Mum and Dad exchange smiles.

'Only you,' says Dad, 'could call Weston Manor, "just a house". Take another look, Tabitha.'

I scowl at him using my real name and glare up at the house in front of us. Yeah, it's kind of smart, I suppose. It's probably more of a mansion than a house. Elegant, painted white with dark green shutters and great long glass windows running along a verandah on each side. There are smaller windows up on the top floor and a wing on each side of the house with a pointed gable on top.

'Emma says the servants lived in one of those wings,' says Mum, following my gaze.

Emma Houghton is the head of museums and galleries at Weston Borough Council. She's the one who has arranged for Dad to take the job of curator.

I glance at Mum where she's gathering her bags up in the front seat of the car.

She still looks like a dancer even though she's dressed in a fleece and combats. Her hair is tied back into a loose ponytail and wisps of her glossy brown hair hang around her face so that she resembles one of those old-fashioned women in paintings. She's thin – you can see her cheekbones trying to cut through her fair skin.

'What's that?' I say, pointing at a flight of white concrete steps in the middle of the grass. 'How can they be stairs? They don't go anywhere!'

Mum smiles. 'That was where the ladies of the manor would mount their horses,' she says.

'So that they didn't have to leap up from the ground and ruin their long dresses.'

I pull a face.

'Weird,' I say.

Dad is getting out of the car and stretching, even though we've only come a few miles.

'I think the first thing I'll do is find a kettle and make some tea,' he says, rubbing his eyes and blinking.

Mum nods in agreement.

'Come on,' she says. 'Your nose has stopped bleeding now. Get out of the car.'

She addresses her remark to me, but Ben's the one who needs to be told the most. He's now fiddling about with the electric button on the car window, lost in his own little world as usual.

I shove him with my foot until he shoots me a sullen look and slides out of the car on the other side.

Mum, Dad and Ben stand for a moment in front of the house, gazing up at the dark windows with shutters pulled across them. Dad has his arm draped over Mum's shoulders. Ben stands next to them, very small beside Dad's giant frame. All three of them have the same shiny dark-brown hair. I don't look like them. Mine, for some reason, is as yellow as corn. I've got Dad's skin, though. In summer my cheeks go strawberry red. Mum's the only one who tans.

The house reminds me of a giant white square that's been plonked down in the middle of an enormous green park. It's very quiet. No signs of life; no smoke coming out of the chimneys; no cars or vans or coaches pulling up next to us. The arched gateway leading from the side of the house into the back gardens is padlocked shut. That's because the house isn't open to the public on Sundays, or so Mum has told us way too many times.

Mum and Dad and Ben are still staring up at the house. They look like they are frozen solid, but when I get out of the car Mum turns towards me, smiles and holds out her hand.

Then she turns back to gaze up at the manor like she's in some weird trance or something.

'We're going to be so happy here,' she says. 'I just know it. This is what we all need – a fresh start.'

Dad squeezes her hand when she says this and pulls her closer.

I look up at the dark, unblinking eyes of the house and I get the weirdest feeling.

It's not a good feeling.

It's the feeling of being pulled into something dark by a hand I can't see and not being able to stop it happening even if I want to.

It's like the house is waiting.

Waiting for me to move in.

Chapter One

Dad's new job title is 'Keeper of Weston Manor'.

He used to have another job nearby until the council decided that they couldn't afford to pay him any longer because they needed our flat for offices and storage space.

Dad was worried he'd have to sign on to the dole, but Emma Houghton called him one night and said that after twenty years of having no live-in Keeper, the council had decided that Weston Manor needed one again and that she was keen for somebody with the right experience to take over even though she

9

couldn't offer him as much pay as he got in his last position.

So I guess you could say that this job came up in the nick of time, or else we'd be homeless.

We don't have a house anywhere else.

We used to have a flat in London near to the Royal Ballet when Mum danced there every night. After she retired, there was a long period when she had no work and Dad hadn't yet found his Keeper job and was working as an art historian at a big London museum and it didn't pay enough for us to stay in our beautiful Georgian flat so we sold up and moved in with Gran for a few months until Dad managed to get work.

Mum was a really famous ballet dancer until she got to thirty-eight and decided to retire so that she could devote more time to Ben and me. She never talks about it much, but sometimes I wonder if she wishes she had carried on longer. The time at home didn't exactly work out as she'd planned it.

This new place, Weston Manor, looks kind of OK.

Yeah. I reckon things are going to be better here.

We walk through the grand front door to the manor and Dad flicks switches and lights up the enormous entrance hall.

'It's gorgeous!' says Mum, gazing around with her eyes wide.

'Yeah, yeah,' I mutter. I'm tired and lugging a heavy suitcase. 'Where's our flat?'

Mum and Dad laugh when I say this, but Dad leads us down a long corridor on the ground floor, past two very large grand rooms to a brown front door with a gold doorbell and a plate with our surname on it.

'Here we are,' he says. 'Home sweet home.'
He staggers in holding a box in one hand and
jangling his keys in the other.

Mum puts her bags down. She unpacks the
kettle from the top of the box and heads into
a pleasant, blue-tiled kitchen with a view of
the front drive to Weston. She drifts around
our new flat in the wing of Weston Manor,
inspecting the bedrooms.

'Do you fancy this one, Tabs?' she says,
opening the door to a square, light-filled room
on the second floor. It looks out over the
croquet lawn at the back of the house. 'I think
it used to be a servant's bedroom. Not a bad
size, is it?'

I shrug.

'OK,' I say. But my heart lifts. The room is
really pretty. And it's going to be all mine. I
help Mum carry boxes and suitcases up into
my new room and then she goes downstairs

to choose her and Dad's room and I bounce on the bed a few times and look around my new room.

There's a small white fireplace just by the window and wooden floorboards that have been stripped back and varnished, covered by a thick Indian carpet, with a single bed in the middle of it. The ceiling is bare and white and there's no furniture other than one ancient-looking oak chest of drawers.

I turn the handle of a door and find myself in a tiny adjoining bathroom. There's a deep white bath with enormous gold taps and a toilet with a wooden seat with a chain pull hanging over it. The sash window over the loo has the same view as from the bedroom.

I go back into my room and finish unpacking. I've packed all my make-up and brushes and moisturisers in a little leather bag that Gemma lent me. Gemma's my best mate at school and she looks a lot like a young Cat Deeley which is a bit sick-making. I arrange all the little brushes and compacts and bottles on the oak chest of drawers and then I lie on the bed and stare at the ceiling for a while.

It feels OK, this room. Mum said that the entire wing is much newer than the rest of the house. Before that the servants had to work and sleep in the basement kitchens in the main house, although a couple of the senior maids had bedrooms upstairs near the family and sometimes the junior housemaids had tiny attic rooms right up in the roof.

'Poor things must have been sweltering in summer,' Mum says.

She's always worrying about people, even people who've been dead for decades. Mum's soft hearted. Not like Dad. He's a bit more fiery and opinionated. That's why he makes a good Keeper. He's strict and brilliant at sticking to routines. If Mum was Keeper she'd drift through houses forgetting to lock doors and windows and probably not even notice if an army of burglars marched up the stairs and started helping themselves to the silver.

'Let me help you pack that,' she'd say, offering them boxes and cups of tea.

Ben's airy-fairy, like Mum. He cries all the time and mopes about, not saying much and looking pale.

I'm more like Dad – quick-tempered and impatient.

And different.

I'm not much like the girls in my class at school. Gemma and I have a laugh but even she thinks I'm a bit weird sometimes. There are reasons for that, I guess. But Gem's all right about it. She's a true friend.

I flick the switch on my laptop and sink into retail heaven.

There's a gentle knock on our door just as Mum's toasting up a big plateful of cheese muffins, drenching them in butter because she's decided to have a day off her diet.

'Oh,' I hear Dad say. 'It's good of you to come round so soon.'

He comes into the lounge, stepping over boxes and crates and followed by a huge hulk of a man who has to stoop to avoid bashing his head on the light.

'This is Sid,' says Dad. 'He's head of security here. If you ever see anybody acting suspiciously around the manor, you contact Sid. OK?'

As though I'm planning on spending loads of time snooping around the manor looking for weirdos or something . . .

'Yes,' I say to keep Dad quiet because he's got his manic expression on.

Mum sighs and holds out her hand to Sid.

'Excuse my husband,' she says. 'We're all a bit tired from the move today. What he really should be doing is offering you a drink. Tea? Coffee? And could you manage a muffin?'

Sid's face lights up at the sight of Mum's tea tray and he settles down on the end of the sofa. Ben gives him a look of alarm but then decides he's a friendly sort and stays huddled up on the other end of it with his eyes fixed upon a piece of Lego.

'Don't mind if I do, pet,' Sid says. 'I reckon the old house can look after itself for ten minutes.'

He's smiling at me, so I half-smile back even though what he's saying seems a bit stupid. I mean – how can a house look after itself?

I like Sid's face though. It's round and open and he doesn't have much hair left, only a dark shadow of what was once probably hair even darker than Mum's. He's got one pierced ear with a gold stud in.

Mum passes him a cup of tea and two muffins and he sinks his teeth into the soft bread with a sigh of pleasure.

'I can see I'm going to like you lot living here,' he says. 'It can get a bit – monotonous, this security-guard lark. Nice to have a new family to breathe life into this old house.'

Sid accepts a third muffin from Mum, wolfs it down in about three seconds and drains the bottom of his teacup with a big slurp.

'Right – no rest for the wicked!' he says. 'Which probably explains a lot about this house!'

He laughs a bit at this and then realises we're all staring at him, trying to work out what he means.

'I'm just having a little joke,' he says. 'You'll get used to me. And the house. It's a bit of an acquired taste but it's a beautiful place to live.'

He gets up, blocking all the light from the window with his huge frame and ducks out of the door with a wink and a wave.

After we've washed up and started to put some of our plates and cups away, Ben goes into his new room to play and Mum says that she needs a lie-down. She's got 'depression' and although it isn't so bad any more, she still has to have loads of rests and be careful not to get over-tired, so Dad locks the door of the flat behind us and we walk back down the long corridor that takes us into the heart of the house and we begin a tour of Weston Manor.

It's very dark in the entrance hall.

'It won't be like this during the week,' says Dad. 'Lights, heating and masses of visitors. You must keep out of the way, Tabs. Sid and his staff are very busy.'

'Erm, I won't be here during term time, Dad,' I say, but Dad is flicking switches and throwing all the shadowy chairs, tables and paintings into a sudden pool of golden light.

'Wow,' I say, despite meaning not to. I can't think how I didn't say that when I first came in. The entrance hall is enormous and kind of beautiful. There's a fireplace made of marble and four huge white marble pillars holding up the middle of the room. Masses of silver gleams out from dark oak cupboards and there are paintings hung right round the room.

'That's the lady who owned the house,' says Dad. He's pointing at a large painting of a woman dressed in a long, black Victorian dress and standing sideways so that I can see her severe profile and aristocratic nose. 'Lady Eleanor Thomas-Fulford.'

'Oh,' I say. I'm disappointed. I thought that the beautiful lady in a white ball gown who is smiling out at me from an enormous oil painting by the fireplace might be the owner.

'That was one of her half-sisters, Lucinda,' says Dad, following my gaze. 'She was a twin. The other one was just as beautiful. Rose. You'll probably see some photographs of her as we go around the house.'

He ushers me into a doorway to the left of the entrance hall and clicks another switch.

'This was the original dining room,' says Dad. 'Before it moved into the new wing where we live.'

The room is very dim, even with the lights on. There are heavy oak panels on the walls and gothic chairs and tables to match.

I shiver. 'Bit dark,' I say.

Dad leads me through an adjoining door into a smaller room that is crammed to the hilt with plush chairs and small shining tables. There's a desk in the corner, covered with faded black-and-white photographs of dogs and children. A clock ticks away to itself on the mantelpiece over the fireplace.

It's a cosy room but kind of stuffy.

Like it needs the windows opened wide and a rush of fresh air from the park to come in.

I wander over and stare at some of the photographs.

'This was Lady Eleanor's morning room,' says Dad. He's running his hand over the top of an elaborately embroidered chair seat when he says this.

'She must have been dog mad,' I say, because most of the photos feature the blurry features of long-dead pets.

I love dogs. I'm hoping to persuade Mum and Dad to let me have a puppy once we get settled in.

'Oh yes,' says Dad. 'You ain't seen nothing yet!'

He's enjoying this.

Dad loves old houses the way that other people love chocolate or clothes or train sets or whatever other things they might be obsessed by.

With Dad, it's 'The Past'. He's always going on about it. Sometimes, if I screw up my face and narrow my eyes, I can see Dad in an old-fashioned suit with a handlebar moustache instead of his goatee and with a pair of spectacles held to his piercing blue eyes.

'Come on, Tabs,' says Dad. We pass out of the morning room and back into the entrance hall but not before a tiny mirror in the doorway catches my eye.

'Why would there be a mirror there?' I say. 'Why isn't it inside the room?'

Dad comes back to take a look.

'Not sure,' he says. 'But I'm guessing that

the servants would check their appearance before going in to see to Lady Eleanor. She was very fussy about how they looked, from what I've heard.'

I nod. Kind of makes sense.

We pass in front of the grand staircase and I glance up as we go by. It's very brown. Brown banisters, brown patterned carpet and brown panelled walls that are covered in dark paintings of brown horses and dogs.

'Do you want to go up?' says Dad. 'There are loads of bedrooms up there and another floor in the attic.'

The weird thing is that I love grand staircases and always pretend that I'm some elegant lady coming down them in a ball gown.

But I don't want to go up this one.

I look up it a bit more and then my appetite kicks in like I haven't eaten for a year and it's all I can think of.

'Could we just do downstairs?' I say to Dad. 'I'm hungry.'

Just as I say this, the waft of eggs and bacon comes through from somewhere and my stomach growls with happy anticipation of Mum's dinner.

I move away back through the entrance hall and Dad shows me the grand dining room near the entrance to our flat with its odd bookcases full of white, Chinese porcelain lions and then the elegant drawing room – the largest room downstairs – with two grand fireplaces, a crystal chandelier hanging down in the middle and floor-to-ceiling green shutters. Dad flings these open to reveal the back grounds of the manor and a view of the tiny medieval parish church that sits just to the left of the house.

By the time we've gone down into the basement of the main house and looked at the old kitchens and the scullery and the butler's pantry and the housemaid's parlour and the line of old bells, which still hang in the corridor waiting in vain for the lady of the manor to ring them and get the servants rushing upstairs, I'm tired out and starving.

It's been a long day of moving and packing and getting used to new things.

'You look like I feel,' says Dad as we head back down the long corridor on the ground floor that leads to the brown wooden door of our flat with 'Grey' on the gold plate just next to the bell.

I glance at my reflection in the glass of the long conservatory windows as we pass them and it seems Dad is right.

My fair hair's all lank and limp and my face is pale with dark rings under the eyes.

I look about ninety-three instead of fourteen. Great.

And I'm supposed to be seeing Jake

tomorrow night. I've been going out with him for nearly six months and he's only like the hottest boy on the entire planet. He'd been pestering me to go out with him for ages before that and he's still really keen. Gemma says he's obsessed with me!

Mum doesn't like me going out on school nights but tough.

I'll tell Ben to keep Mum company while I'm out and while Dad's patrolling the manor and making sure everything has been prepared for the next day of visitors.

Not that Ben's much company. He's only five. And he doesn't have much confidence, unlike me. Dad says I've got too much.

Ben would burst into tears if he even saw his own shadow.

I burst through the door with my tongue practically hanging out from starvation.

'We're back! Let's have dinner!' I yell, but there's silence.

Dad pokes his head into the darkened bedroom he's going to share with Mum and I hear him murmuring in a low voice before he comes back out into the lounge again looking a bit worried.

'Mum's got one of her heads,' he says. 'So I'm going to pop to the parade over the road and see if I can get us a takeway, OK?'

I start to speak and then stop again. Maybe Mum started dinner and then her head got worse again and she had to lie down.

I go into the modern kitchen, which has been fitted by the council for our tenancy. The room is cold and the fridge is full of stuff but I can't see any bacon.

I peer in the bin but there's nothing in there, not even a bin liner.

Oh well.

Ben creeps out of his bedroom and puts his arms around my leg. He looks frightened, like he doesn't want to be here. We've had a lot of changes in our life over the last few years.

'Don't worry,' I say. 'It will be OK. This is a nice house. Everything will be fine. And Mum will get happier. You'll see.'

Ben looks up at me with his dark eyes and gives me the tiniest smile, so I let him explore my new bedroom. He sits on the bed and watches me try out new eyeshadows and we both try not to hear Mum moaning in pain through the wall. When Dad finally comes back I jump a mile at the sound of his key in the lock and then my heart leaps with relief at the smell of prawn crackers and black-bean noodles, and Mum comes out of her room and manages to eat with us and, although it's not quite like I imagined it being on the first night, it's kind of OK and we're together.

'So do you like Weston?' Dad says as we finish with a tub of vanilla ice cream from a late-night shop that Dad found next to the takeaway. His eyes are all lit up and eager as he waits for my reply.

'Yeah,' I say. 'Yeah. I think I'm going to enjoy it.'

There's a sharp laugh. Right in my ear.

I jump and shake my head like I'm trying to get a wasp off it.

It must have been Dad. He's good at projecting his voice, after all. He used to give talks at the museum and it still shows.

I'm tired, right? It's been a long day.

'I'm going to bed,' I say. 'Night.'

Ben's eyes follow me as I leave the room. I wonder if he'll come and get in my bed in the middle of the night?

He usually does.

Chapter Two

On Monday morning I wake up and forget where I am.

I'd got so used to my last bedroom in our flat with its thick red curtains and cream walls that for a moment I gaze around this bare white room and can't think what has just happened.

Then Mum bangs on my bedroom door and shouts, 'Tabitha, get up or I'm going to come in and drag you out of that bed!' and my mind kind of kicks into gear. With a butterfly thrill in my stomach I remember that I've got my date with Jake later and that we're living in a beautiful manor house now.

Right.

The date calls for extra attention to my appearance.

Can't get out of wearing school uniform for the day but at least I can make my hair look good.

I go into the little bathroom that adjoins my room and lean over the deep white bath to wash my hair in some special blonde stuff that Mum got me.

It's cold in here. White tiled walls, green tiled floor and a draught blowing under the little sash window overlooking the back lawn.

Can't have been much fun for the servant who lived in this part of the house. At least in my room there's a warm radiator so that I can huddle by it while I'm drying my hair. I tip my head upside down and blow heat on to my roots. My hair's really fine, which is annoying, but there's plenty of it.

I draw a layer of eyeliner inside my eyelids and stand back to survey the results in the mirror. The black of the eyeliner makes my eyes seem more blue than usual.

I put in a pair of blue stud earrings (we're not allowed to wear dangly ones) and spray a load of gloss stuff all over my head.

'It will have to do,' I say to my reflection.

Ben comes in and gazes up at me, so I ruffle his hair.

'Mum will kill me if I don't hurry,' I say. 'See you later.'

Ben doesn't have to go to school. He's too unwell for proper school. Besides, I don't think he'd get on too well with all the other crazy noisy kids.

I eat cereal in the kitchen with Mum and Dad, and Sid pops in again, jangling an enormous bunch of keys which he puts on the breakfast table. Dad picks up that huge bunch of keys with a glint in his eye while Mum is clearing up the breakfast things. I kiss my parents goodbye and come out of our flat. For the first time, I go on my own down the long corridor past the manor's dining room and drawing room and into the grand entrance hall.

It looks different today.

All the shutters are drawn back to let the sunlight stream in and the heaters are pumping out hot air so that the oil paintings on the wall sway and bump on their long wires.

I glance at the glamorous portrait of Lucinda MacDonald. In the daylight her white dress glows less. Other portraits I haven't noticed seem to swim into view as I look around the room. There's one of a kind-looking old man with a grey beard and another of a man who resembles him but looks younger and less friendly. This man is wearing some sort of soldier's uniform and has black eyes and a dark moustache. He glares out of the picture at me.

'That's Captain Jack,' announces a woman's voice.

There's a lady in a dark uniform and white shirt stacking postcards on the reception desk. She looks old – about thirty or so. She smiles at me as I walk towards her.

'He was a funny piece of work,' she says. 'Lady Eleanor's only son. Always up to mischief. He never inherited this place, thank God.'

I smile because I don't know what she's talking about.

'You must be Tabitha,' she says. Her dark eyes dance. 'We were told that the new family were moving in this weekend. I'm Dawn.'

I reach over the desk piled up with brochures and cards and shake her hand.

'I do the tickets here,' she says. 'And sometimes I'm on security. We all just muck in and do whatever needs doing. You'll get used to us being around.'

I smile at her and hover for a bit. Then I glance at my watch.

'I'm late for school,' I say. 'See you later.'

I push open the heavy front door of Weston Manor, run past the Edwardian shoe-scraper and the old-fashioned bell pull and down the tall flight of white stone steps. There are cars pulling up in the horseshoe-shaped drive and other members of staff are getting out of them but I haven't got time to speak to anyone else so I leg it out of the grounds and down Weston Drove towards the bus stop.

It's only as I get on the bus, finding my seat next to Gemma as it drives back up past the entrance to the manor, that I look at the house and get a little thrill in my bones as I see it sitting there all white and quiet.

'Did you know that I live there now?' I say to Olivia White, one of my so-called other friends from school.

She shoots me a scornful look. 'So?' she says. 'It's just a house. And my mum says it's really weird and she wouldn't want to live there anyway.'

I sink into my seat feeling a bit deflated even though Gemma whispers to me to ignore Olivia because she's the biggest bitch out there.

I miss my last home. I miss my old bedroom and the private garden that we had there, and even though life wasn't perfect I kind of see what Gran is saying when she says things like, 'Better the Devil you know.'

I've left so many good things behind me.

*

School seems to drag on for years.

Then again, it always does when you're impatient for something to happen later on.

I sit through maths, chemistry, English and religious studies and me and Gemma text like mad underneath the desk all day, and then finally the bell rings and I go to the loo with Gemma to get ready for my date with Jake.

'Shame about the gross dress,' she comments as we peer at my reflection in the grimy mirrors in the school loo.

It's May so I'm wearing my blue school dress with the short sleeves, which is kind of vile, but we both know that if I flout the school rules and get seen outside in my own clothes then my life won't be worth living.

'You can borrow these if you like,' says Gemma. She pours a slinky armful of blue jangly bracelets on to my thin wrist and I clink my arm up and down, enjoying the feeling of cold metal.

'Ah, thanks,' I say. 'They match my earrings! You're a mate.'

I smile at Gem in the mirror. She's kind of kept me going over the past few years when things have been tough at home. She has a friendly round face, long wavy hair and big sky-coloured eyes. We look about as different to one another as two people could possibly look.

'And your hair,' says Gemma. She pushes my head upside down into the sink and sprays a load of volume stuff all over it. When I tip my head back up my long blonde hair has got new layers in it and falls in a dishevelled mess all over my shoulders.

'Nice,' I say. 'Thanks.'

Then she runs off home and leaves me pretending to be cool and disinterested just outside the school gates.

Jake's already there, with his hands in his pockets. He's whistling all casual, like he's forgotten I'm due, but when I go up to him he flushes and pecks me on my cheek and gives me one of his cute soppy looks.

'All right,' he says. 'D'you want a pizza or a curry or something?'

My heart kind of sinks a bit. It's hardly the most romantic declaration of undying love ever. And I am kind of a romantic. Mum says I watch too many slushy American films and I know deep down that they're rubbish, but after the last few years it feels like good escapism from everything that's going on in my life. I like all those films where a boy meets a girl and they almost get it together but they don't and there turns out to be some reason, like one of them is a vampire or suffering from a terminal illness.

'Intelligent girl like you should watch decent films,' Dad is always saying to me. I sigh and stuff my fingers in my ears.

Thing is, I know he's right. I get high marks at school.

But being clever only ever seems to land me in trouble.

So I watch trashy films and read romantic books and they kind of dull things down and make me feel safe.

Or that's the plan.

Jake takes me to a pizza place in town. It's really noisy and full of babies crying and toddlers having parties so it's quite difficult to hear what he's saying, but I enjoy looking at his gelled-up hair and his blue eyes and tanned skin, and as usual he gives me masses of attention and doesn't even look when a gang of really pretty blonde girls come in for a party, pushing past our table in their summer tops and leggings. I keep reminding myself that he IS one of the hottest boys in school and I'm so busy staring at him that I don't hear what he's asking me for a moment before I realise he's asking me about the manor.

'I said, did you know that my gran won't go in there?' he says. 'She reckons it's kind of spooky inside.'

I laugh in what I hope is a cool and casual way, pulling all my long hair to one side and arranging it over one shoulder.

'Yeah, it's maybe a bit weird,' I say. The voice sounds as if it's coming from somebody else, somebody all grown-up and sophisticated. 'But actually it's really cool living in a manor.'

I hear myself say all this and Jake's smiling away so I must be doing a convincing job. But inside there's a tiny sinking feeling of doubt.

Somehow I get Jake off the subject and I

ask him loads of stuff about himself and he goes a bit red when he gives me the answers. It's nice seeing how much he likes me, so for a few more hours I forget about my new home and Mum's migraines and sadness and Ben's scared look, and I just enjoy having Jake give me lots of attention.

When it gets to seven I stand up and brush crumbs from my school uniform.

'I'd better get back,' I say. 'Mum worries if I'm late.'

The light is fading as I get on the bus. Jake watches and waves from the pavement and I half-wave but inside I feel a bit embarrassed, even though we have been together for months. As the bus pulls into Weston Drove and I get off to walk the last little bit, I get the sinking feeling again, like I'm about to do an exam or something. It gets worse as I walk up the horseshoe drive to the manor. All the visitors have long since gone and the shutters are closed in every window. The house stares down at me with those dark, unblinking eyes. I climb the white stone steps and push twice on the bell like I've agreed with Dad so that he'll come and walk me back to our flat.

While I'm waiting for him to let me in, I glance over to the ruined stable buildings on the right and for just a second I imagine them as they once were, rushing with life and noise. Horses pulling carriages, grooms brushing them down and stabling them. I swear I can almost smell the stench of horse dung and blocked drains and a whiff of something sweeter – peaches, perhaps, or grapes? – and then Dad's pulling open the heavy front door and giving me a hug and all of that sort of melts away when I smell his warm jumper and the deodorant he always uses.

I hold on to him tight until he moves away

to pull down a blind in the entrance hall.

Then something makes me jump.

I don't know what, at first.

Then it's there. A feeling at the back of my head. Like a pack of ice has been pressed against it. 'Ow,' I say, clapping my hand under the nape of my neck.

I twist round to look behind, out over the semi-circular drive with the weird flight of steps that go nowhere.

Nothing.

Dad's not listening. He's jingling his keys and looking around the entrance hall. 'Quite a place to live, Tabs,' he says as he locks the big front door behind me.

'Yeah', I say. He's right. The house does look beautiful as we walk down the long corridor to our flat. But I can't concentrate on looking at the things Dad points out to me.

The moon shines through the windows of

the glass verandah and lights up bits and pieces of furniture in the drawing room and dining room as we pass by their doorways.

I don't want to look but something in me can't seem to stop.

That's why, as Dad is pulling out the key to our flat and inserting it in the lock, I'm still standing by the dining-room door peering into the gloom. It's very still inside. I can see the outline of the great polished table. The white faces of the Chinese lions glint in the moonlight from their dark mahogany cases.

There's something else too. At the far end of the dining-room table, on one of the high-backed gothic chairs. I strain my eyes, trying to see.

'Come in, Tabs,' says Dad, already inside our flat.

'OK,' I reply.

I turn to leave and follow Dad but I have to

look back. I don't want to. I just have to.

There's nothing there.

A wave of tiredness hits me. I can hardly drag my feet over to our flat.

'Come inside, Tabitha,' orders Dad.

He shuts our door and bolts us safe inside.

Chapter Three

Mum's dancing again.

Well, she's not dancing for an audience at Covent Garden any more, but Dad's rigged her up a barre in our flat in the huge basement room which was once the servants' kitchen and is now a storage area for council files, folders and furniture. He clears a big space by the wall and drills holes into it to fit the shiny barre. Then he puts up a long mirror and installs some little spotlights in the ceiling so that they can shine down on Mum and she can see what she's doing.

At first Mum's not keen about going down

to the basement and dancing there while we're all upstairs doing other things, but after a few sessions she starts to look forward to it.

Sometimes I creep halfway down the stairs and sit there hugging my knees so that I can watch.

Mum dances like she's trying to reach something.

Or someone.

Her arms stretch out towards things that I can't see and her face is filled with this strange yearning look that she doesn't use in our normal everyday life. When she pirouettes round in circles her limbs end up folded around her and she hugs her own elbows to finish, like she's trying to hibernate away from the world.

Sometimes she just puts her leg up on the barre and examines her legs and her feet in their narrow pointe shoes and I can tell she's missing the discipline of her Royal Ballet training and maybe wondering whether she gave it all up too early.

Dad never interrupts Mum when she's dancing.

He's got about a million and one jobs to do around the manor and his latest project is to update the guidebook for visitors, which means taking a thorough inventory of every single piece of furniture and every ornament on display in the house.

'It's going to take me about a year just to do that,' he complains, but I can tell he's really enjoying himself. He gets up early with a determined glint in his eye and bounds off into the main house every day with a laptop and a big wad of paper, and sometimes he even forgets to come back for lunch and doesn't reappear until the manor has been shut and it's dark outside.

It's half term so I get a whole week off school to hang around and annoy Mum.

'Why don't you go and help your father?' she says. She's chosen today as the day she's going to paint our kitchen and hang new curtains in my bedroom.

I pull a face. 'It's cosier in the flat,' I say. I'm lying about on the sofa in our lounge with my legs in thick stripy socks and my hair all un-brushed and un-washed.

I love half term but after being freaked out a couple of weeks ago I don't have any urge to go into the main part of Weston Manor. Plus I've got other things on my mind. I think about Jake a lot. Can't stop thinking about him.

When I lie in my square white room at night, the outside light is illuminating the fireplace and the wooden boards and I'm wondering a bit about the servant who once slept in this room, Jake's face somehow cuts through my wonderings and banishes them all away so that I'm left with this really cool image of his smooth cheeks and deep blue eyes giving me that intense stare.

But it's weird. I like him more when I'm imagining him. When I actually stand next to him at school I feel kind of half-pleased and half-irritated. And it's always a relief when it's just me and Gem and I can be myself.

'Go on, Tabitha,' Mum is saying. 'Please. I need to get things done before I'm struck with another of my heads.'

She does look a bit flushed and tired so I swing my legs off the back of the sofa and slouch off to get showered and dressed.

From my little tiled bathroom I can see the old walled garden of the manor. Dad says that there are these tiny gravestones belonging to all the old manor pets out there so I decide that I might as well go and take a look at them later.

It's still early.

I take a deep breath and open the door to our flat, then go down the long corridor into the main part of the house.

I don't much want to look at the dining room but something compels me to anyway. In the daylight everything looks normal. Sunlight glints off the silver candlesticks on the table. The high-backed chairs sit to attention around the long polished table. The room smells of flowers and wax polish and the security guard, Sid, has already been round and thrown open the green shutters so that light pours into the room from all directions.

'Tabsy, you're an idiot,' I say to myself.

I walk around the room once, just to prove

to myself that there's nothing to be scared of.

Then I head into the entrance hall.

Sid is behind the reception desk setting up the computer to connect to the security cameras. There are cameras in every room of the manor, just in case any visitors fancy helping themselves to the valuables.

'Morning pet!' he booms at me.

Dawn looks up. She's stacking postcards again and tearing tickets off a long roll in preparation for the visitors. Two of them have been allowed in early and are standing chatting by the fireplace.

'Hiya, Tabitha!' Dawn says, her dark eyes sparkling. 'Don't suppose you want to give me a hand, do you?'

I smile.

'Maybe later,' I say. 'Going to find Dad.'

'He's upstairs,' says Dawn. 'In Lady Eleanor's bedroom, I think.'

I thank her and head off towards the staircase, saying 'good morning' to the two old lady visitors as I pass the fireplace.

They both nod at me and return to their conversation.

They're dressed in short, smart dark suits and have patent-leather heels and perfectly groomed white hair in buns.

I smile. They look kind. Then I head up the stairs to find Dad.

The staircase at Weston Manor is kind of creepy.

It's the only time I've been up it on my own.

At the foot of the stairs is an arched glass cupboard built into the wall. It's full of little porcelain shepherdesses.

Dad told me that there was a doorway here in the old days and that the cupboard has only been put in quite recently.

I stand looking in at the little china figures for a moment but then I start to shiver. It's not the sort of cold feeling I get on a biting winter's day – the sort that gives you flushed cheeks and numb fingers. And it's not the sort of shivering I get just before coming down with flu, when my cheeks burn up red and I can't stop shaking.

No – it's more a sort of bone cold.

It starts from my feet and moves up my legs and into my chest before causing my face to chill.

I run my hand along my arm.

It's cold and clammy, and the hairs are standing on end.

I can still hear Dawn talking on the telephone in the entrance hall, even though I can't see her and it's kind of comforting, so I tell myself to stop being silly and I move away from the arch and run upstairs to find Dad.

He's in Lady Eleanor's bedroom, the second room on the right at the top of the stairs. All the bedrooms are on this floor, separated by a small square landing on which a grandfather clock ticks away the seconds. I poke my head inside the room.

Dad's got his tape measure out and is measuring the four-poster bed that sits right in the centre of the room. 'I don't think that this is the original bed,' he says, more to himself than to me. 'The Victorians preferred brass beds. Stopped insects eating the wood. I reckon that this one was put in later on.'

I step into the middle of the room and look around. It's light and airy, with floral curtains tied back by long red velvet sashes and an oval dressing table with a mirror just underneath the windows. The bed takes up most of the room. It has a floral bedspread, which matches the curtains, and there's a long plush sofa along the foot of the bed and a mahogany chest of drawers near to the door.

'Who's that?' I say, peering at a large photograph of a man that perches on the chest. He looks kind of familiar. Dark eyes, moustache, portly stomach bulging out over his waistband.

'Captain Jack,' says Dad with one end of the measuring tape between his teeth and the other end stretched up one of the bed's wooden posts. 'Eleanor's only son. I don't think she liked him very much.'

'Why?' I say, but Dad has moved over to the window and is gazing out over the overgrown lawns and messy walled garden at the back of the house. I can see that he's planning to take on more gardening staff and knock the entire place into shape, so I leave him in Lady Eleanor's bedroom and go back on to the landing.

There are lots of other bedrooms to explore up here but somehow I don't feel like going into them on my own.

Dawn's laugh wafts up the stairs and I follow it down.

Sid is standing by the main door jingling his keys, about to unlock it and let the public in.

'Time to let in the great unwashed!' he says as I emerge from the foot of the stairs and round the corner into the entrance hall.

'Sid,' says Dawn. 'That's not a very nice way to refer to visitors. Without them the council would shut this house and you'd be out of a job.'

I look over to the fireplace. 'Those lady visitors looked very clean,' I say. 'Did they already go? They must have rushed round the house at top speed.'

Dawn looks over to where I'm standing.

'Visitors?' she says. 'They're all outside, love. Look.'

There's a long queue of impatient-looking people in spring dresses and flip-flops all shifting about and peering through the windows.

I laugh.

'Not them!' I say. 'The two old ladies who were chatting by the fireplace!'

Sid turns round sharply when I say this. He glances at Dawn.

Her smile has faded but she continues to speak in the same low, pleasant voice that she always uses. 'Oh of course,' she says, holding her reel of tickets in front of her. 'I forgot I'd let them in!'

Sid has turned away from me and is fiddling about with the computer on the reception desk.

'I'd forget my head if it wasn't bolted on

to my shoulders!' Dawn is saying.

Something's not right, but I decide to leave them to it.

As I head back through the entrance hall, I run my finger along the edge of the white marble fireplace.

'See you later, Tabs!' calls Dawn as I walk towards the flat.

I turn round to wave but she's deep in conversation with Sid. I strain my ears as I walk in slow-motion towards the door of our flat but I can't really hear what they're saying.

Then they realise that I'm still there and they open the grand doors to let the visitors pour through.

I go back inside to find Mum.

Chapter Four

When Dad comes home that evening I tell him about how Dawn forgot she'd let two old ladies in. Dad ruffles my hair like I'm about six and gives his deep laugh.

'I wouldn't trust that Dawn!' he says. 'I hear she's got a bit of a reputation for mucking about. She was pulling your leg, I bet.'

Actually I wouldn't bet. Dawn didn't look like she was pulling my leg. She looked as if she was covering something up. I don't tell Dad that, though. Dad is one of the least mysterious people in the world. He's got a scientific explanation for everything that happens and he refuses to entertain any other theories.

Mum is cooking sausage and chips while I'm telling Dad about the women but I can tell from her shoulders that she's listening to every word.

'Don't be so mistrustful of poor Dawn,' she says to Dad. 'People are entitled to make mistakes now and again. Even you!'

'Ow!' I yell. Ben has just bitten my leg underneath the table.

Mum gives me a look. 'Lay the table, Tabitha, and get the ketchup,' is all she says, but over the meal I catch her giving me the odd worried glance when she thinks I'm not looking.

Mum's very protective. She's always watching me and wondering where I am.

Of course I do the same with Ben. He's my little brother so I have to look out for him, even though he's a pain most of the time.

Like now, when he's trying to pinch chips off my plate.

'Stop it!' I yell before I can help myself.

Mum sighs and buries her head in her hands. 'I just wanted a fresh start here,' she says in the low voice, which I know is going to rise up into hysteria if Dad doesn't somehow find a way to stop it. 'Is that too much to ask? Can't we all just enjoy living in this house without making up stories about old ladies and yelling and making a fuss?'

Dad offers me more sausages. 'Nobody's pretending anything, Rachel,' he says. 'And we ARE enjoying living in the manor. Aren't we, Tabs?'

I nod, stuffing in chips as fast as possible so that I can go upstairs and see if Jake has texted me.

'Tabitha is still pretending, aren't you, Tabitha?' says Mum. Her voice is going all high and squeaky. Uh-oh. Danger alert.

Dad pours her a glass of wine and gives her a long look with his eyebrows raised. The look says, 'Don't start this again.'

'Tabitha is doing very well,' he says. 'She's going to help me with some more of the inventory tomorrow. So you can practise your dancing or go shopping or clean or whatever you want to do.'

I know he means this in a nice way but it comes out kind of patronising and Mum's cheeks flare into angry pink spots.

'Oh, and that's my life now, is it?' she says. 'Shopping, cleaning and a nice little hobby down in the damp old basement while you get obsessed with your new job, just like always?'

She gets up and shoves the plates into the sink, goes upstairs and slams her bedroom door.

Ben jumps at the noise and his dark brown

eyes look up at me, all serious and scared.

I sigh. 'I thought I was supposed to be the moody one,' I venture but Dad glowers at me, so I shut up and eat a hard banana in silence.

Great. Some half term this is turning out to be.

The next day the house is open to the public by the time Dad and I leave our flat and head down the corridor. The dining room is full of light and no visitors have yet made it to that part of the manor. I glance into the huge drawing room as we pass by and admire the heavy crystal chandeliers and the ornate gold mirrors over the two large fireplaces, one on each side of the room. There is a large cabinet full of green and blue Wedgwood vases that I hadn't noticed before, so I stop for a moment to look at it. Gran collects Wedgwood so I always recognise it.

'Come on,' says Dad, already pounding through the entrance hall. 'Morning!' he booms to Dawn who's selling brochures to a small group of students. He gives her his dazzling grin.

'Hi,' she says back. Her short hair is dark and thick against the white shirt of her uniform. She watches Dad's retreating back for a moment as he starts to bound up the grand staircase, two steps at a time. Then she sees me and clears her throat. She gives me a wink before returning to the students.

Dad is working upstairs in the library on the first floor today. It's opposite Lady Eleanor's bedroom and all the time I'm in the library I keep looking across the landing like I'm expecting somebody to come out of there or something. But of course nobody does and instead a stream of visitors go in there, exclaiming with pleasure at the ornate bed and the beautiful paintings and photographs on the wall.

The library is kind of strange.

'It doesn't feel like a library,' I say to Dad. There are loads of books on dark shelves across the entire length of one wall but it still doesn't really look like I'd imagine a library in a manor house to look. There's very little furniture in the room other than a small round rosewood table in the middle and a fireplace with a fender and one or two small ornaments above it.

'That's because it wasn't,' replies Dad. He's busy noting down the titles of the books in the cabinet. 'It used to be a guest bedroom, back in the Victorian era. But nobody would sleep in here because they reckoned it was haunted. More likely damp, in my opinion!'

He gives his great earthy laugh and continues his job.

I go over to the sash window and stare out at the parkland behind the house.

'Why are they playing that?' I say, pointing to a group of women who are hitting balls through small hoops on the ground. The balls clack and clunk together.

'Oh, the manor lets people pay to come and play croquet here,' says Dad. 'But it's not the season yet so perhaps they're just practising. It's usually children who come and copy the croquet scene out of *Alice in Wonderland*.'

'Right,' I say, turning back to the window. I look for children, but can't see any. There are only the three women hitting balls through hoops. Two of them are young and pretty with blonde hair piled up on top of their heads and they're messing about a bit with each other. The other is much older and moving like her bones are made of china. Her hair is silver-grey against her dark dress.

The sun beats down on the croquet lawn and glints off the metal hoops, and for a moment I'm so dazzled by brightness that I shade my eyes with my hand. When I can see the lawn again, the hoops are still there but the women have gone.

'They didn't stay long,' I say to Dad but he's not really listening. Instead he's flicking through an old book with a red cover that he's just found in the bookcase.

'This is fascinating!' he says. 'I don't think it should really still be in the house. I ought to take it to the council archives. Look!'

He passes me the red book. It's got a gold-printed title on the front cover: *A History of Weston Manor by Sir Charles Thomas-Fulford, 1905.*

'That's the man who used to own the house,' says Dad. 'Lady Eleanor's husband. I had no idea he wrote a history of this house!'

I smile. Dad's face is all lit up with excitement and he can't keep still, shifting from leg to leg and fiddling with his hands.

I guess that Dad's having what he often refers to as 'the researcher's high' which he's always telling us is far more thrilling than drugs or alcohol or anything like that.

I glance outside again.

The three women are back. They have stopped playing croquet and are standing in a line facing the back of the house.

They are looking up at me.

Yes – I'm sure of it. But why would they?

Two of them are smiling. The older one isn't. The air around me fills up with the strong scent of lavender.

'Dad,' I begin, but my head is spinning with the sickly sweet smell. The walls of the room start to move in on me. I can hear Dad's voice coming from a long way away, all concerned and serious, but I can't work out where I am any longer and all I can smell is lavender and I can see the croquet lawn up close and larger now and the three women are back again with their mallets and long dresses and I'm right in the middle of their game and the older woman looks straight at me and holds out her thin arms and then I'm back in the library except the ceiling is spinning round and round in circles and then my head bangs back on to the parquet floor and I open my eyes and everything goes still.

'Tabs!' yells Dad. 'Are you all right? What happened?'

I sit up, clutching my head. 'Not sure,' I say. 'There was this really strong smell.'

Dad has gone white. 'You gave me a fright,' he says. 'You just fell straight down. Stay there. I'm going to run to reception and get Sid.'

I open my mouth to protest but he's

thundered off down the staircase and I don't much feel like standing up on my wobbly legs, so instead I sit up on the floor.

The room swims up to swallow me in a coat of blackness and this time I know I'm not going to beat it. I lie down and feel my heart beating in my mouth and the blood rushing around my ears and pouring down the back of my throat.

Oh great, I think. *Another nosebleed.*

Then – nothing.

Chapter Five

When I wake up Dad is looming over me and next to him is the round and slightly sweaty face of Sid.

'How are you feeling, lass?' he says. I reckon that it's a pretty stupid question, given that I'm lying on a hard floor in a smelly library with a pounding headache and Dad shining his torch into my eyes to check for concussion, but I guess Sid's just trying to be kind so I lurch to my feet, steady myself on the edge of the small rosewood table and stuff a tissue up my nose.

'Where did those women go?' I say.

Dad frowns. 'Women?' he says. 'Do you mean the people outside practising croquet? They've probably gone home.'

'I'm sure they were looking at me,' I say.

Sid looks like he's about to speak but then he changes his mind and pulls the blind down on the window instead.

'Gets hot in here,' is all he says.

Dad is running his hands through his hair. 'Hmm,' he says. 'I'm not sure what's happened here but I think you may have had a bit too much heat and excitement today, Tabs. Maybe you're not as well as we thought. Time to get you back to the flat.'

I roll my eyes behind his back. Heat and excitement. Yeah, sure. Like this house is ever HOT, for starters. And I'm not exactly excited.

More like anxious.

And confused.

Sid goes back downstairs and joins Dawn at

reception and Dad escorts me down the stairs and along the ground-floor corridor, like I'm an invalid or something, pointing out all the steps and uneven floor.

'That's it,' he keeps saying. 'Take it easy.'

'Dad,' I say. 'I'm fine. It's no big deal.'

As we pass the reception desk Dawn looks up and catches my eye.

She doesn't say a word.

I think Dawn knows stuff about this house.

Dad walks past the entrance to the grand drawing room, which is now heaving with groups of art students all sketching the ornaments and furniture and it's kind of reassuring to see normal people walking about, so I feel a bit better.

Then we pass the dining-room door but there's only one person in there, a woman in a dark blue dress sitting at the far end of the room by the servants' door.

She's got her head in her hands so I'm about to tell Dad that there's a visitor not feeling very well in the dining room but as I pass by she looks up and stares straight at me.

Bolts of electricity run up and down my spine and a strange buzzing noise fills the air.

Her face is a pale white oval. She has two dark slits for eyes.

I taste blood at the back of my throat. I scream out. 'Dad!'

Dad scoops me under his arm and hustles me into the flat. The sound of our flat door closing behind us is the best sound I have ever heard in my life.

Chapter Six

I'm not allowed out for the rest of that day, or the one after.

My head's pounding and I can't sleep. I keep seeing the faces of old women and younger women and they've all got dark eyes, which bore straight through my head and into my soul, like they know everything I'm thinking.

Jake's sent about fifty million texts asking if I'm OK. I reckon Gemma must have told him I'm ill, cos I didn't actually tell him myself.

Mum insists that a doctor comes to check me out as soon as I get back in the flat after my weird morning with Dad.

'I'm fine,' I say. 'Honest.'

'Tabitha,' she snaps. 'You're having a nosebleed. You're not fine at all. Lean forwards and hold your nose.'

Actually she's right. I'm not fine.

I'm a bit freaked out. But something tells me not to go on about it all to Mum.

She already thinks I'm a bit crazy and unhinged, and the last thing I need is for her to send me off to some mad-person's hospital or something.

So I keep quiet when Mum's around, and Dad's too busy and too much in the real world to try and discuss these things with, so I just sit tucked up on the sofa next to Ben. I wouldn't tell him things, of course, as he's only five and I don't want to scare him, but I think he kind of gets that I'm terrified because his little hand creeps into mine and we watch some rubbish on CBBC together without him saying a word.

The doctor comes and shines yet another torch in my eyes and asks me stupid questions about what year it is and what day it is and I get them all right so he tells Mum to keep me on the sofa for a couple of days and not to have any more 'excitement'.

I wish people wouldn't keep going on about 'excitement'.

Excitement is not banging your head on a hard wooden floor and seeing strange women who aren't really there.

No.

Excitement is Christmas or birthdays or new clothes or going to a gig.

So I spend two days in my pyjamas in our flat while Mum fusses about making me milk jellies (yuk!) and chicken soup (vile) and making me drink fizzy aspirin (grosser than gross).

Gemma comes round to see me. I don't think she's ever been in the manor before because her eyes are even bigger than usual and she's all flushed with excitement when she's let into our flat.

'You're so lucky, Tabs!' she says as I make her a coffee and flop back on to the sofa. Ben shuffles up to the very end to make room for Gemma. I think he likes her cos he always goes quiet and kind of gooey-eyed when she's around. She *is* very pretty. But the good thing is that she doesn't make a big thing of it. She's really into her sport and spends most of her spare time playing in hockey and netball matches right across the county.

'You look rough,' she offers now. I pass her a tube of digestive biscuits and we dunk them into our coffee. 'What've you got? Is it that virus going round?'

I give a small snort at that. I quite fancy

having something as uncomplicated as a virus.

I look at my best friend's smooth healthy face and for a moment I want to tell her everything, offload my worries. She IS my best mate, after all.

But Gem's so much in the real world. Her life is based round sport and horses and dance classes and her family are quite religious and spend every Sunday at church and helping out in the Sunday school.

Still . . .

I decide to try it. She's nice, Gem. She won't make me feel too bad.

'Gem,' I say. 'You know yesterday?'

'Yes,' says Gem, all smart. 'It's the day before today.'

I whack her on the leg and Ben gives a faint smile.

'Well, I kind of saw these three women,' I say. 'Out of the upstairs window. They were playing croquet but they had these weird dresses on.'

'So?' says Gem. She's gazing around our flat, not listening all that much. 'They have croquet days here all the time. My mum's been to one. They probably dress up sometimes.'

'Yeah, I suppose,' I say. It sounds a bit lame now, what I saw, even to me. 'And then later on I saw this other woman sitting in the dining room in a blue dress and she looked up at me and she had this dead sad expression on . . .'

There's a crash in the corridor just outside our front door.

Gem and I jump about fifteen miles in the air.

'What's that?' she says.

'Er, how should I know?' I say.

Only Ben doesn't seem bothered by the noise. He's doing Lego with about a thousand little people dressed up as farmers or policemen.

There's more banging and a weird rustling noise on the wood of the door and we stare at one another for a moment before Mum bursts into the flat with her arms full of broken carrier bags.

'Honestly,' she says. 'They charge you 5p for these bags and then they split about five minutes later! Oh – hello Gemma. Forgot you were coming!'

She struggles through into the kitchen and starts unloading packets of flour and punnets of fruit, so Gemma turns back to me and says:

'Sorry, Tabs – you were telling me something? About a woman in a blue dress in the dining room?'

Mum stops rustling her bags and stares over at me when Gem says that.

'You girls can help me prepare lunch,' she says. Her voice is low but firm.

There's not really any way I can carry on

with my conversation and anyway I can tell that Gem's not that interested, so we chop lettuce, spring onions and tomatoes for the salad Mum's making for lunch.

After Gemma has gone, there's a gentle tap on the door of our flat. Dad goes to open it and Dawn's standing there with a big bag full of grapes.

'Oh,' says Mum, all flustered. 'I must look a state. If I'd known we were expecting a visitor I'd have made myself look a bit more presentable.'

I see Dawn look for the briefest moment at Mum's ripped jeans, baggy sweatshirt and unwashed hair shoved into a messy ponytail, and like loads of people she's wondering how such a famous and beautiful ballerina can have become such a mess. I see Dad looking at Dawn's long skinny legs and I see Mum watching Dad do this. For a moment, I see my Mum as other people see her and I see my Dad being not Dad – not a husband, but a man who still notices other women – and it's like I've started KNOWING all this stuff since I moved into the manor and I never really knew any of it before and I wonder where all this brain power is coming from and why I never had it last year and I'm so busy wondering all this that I fail to thank Dawn, who has put the bunch of grapes next to me on the table.

'Tabitha!' Mum is hissing. 'Manners!'

Dad has already beckoned Dawn to sit next to him on the sofa. He leans back, runs his hand through his hair and gives her his twinkling smile, crossing one leg over the other.

Mum opens a packet of peanuts and tips them with a tinkle into a glass bowl. She pours Dawn a glass of red wine and goes upstairs, coming back two minutes later with a dazzling red lipstick on, her hair combed into a sleek brown bun and wearing a pair of tight black leggings with a floaty pink tunic and a pink wrap tied over the top.

For a moment, Dad loses the thread of his conversation with Dawn and gawps at Mum.

'You look great!' he says and Mum gives him a faint smile, which is the only sort of smile she does these days, and Dawn looks unsettled and glances at her watch.

I can't stop looking at Mum. She's wearing her old rehearsal clothes, but they always look amazing on her.

I look at Dawn. Now I come to think of it, her outfit looks a bit cheap and tight and nasty. Mum looks so classy in her pale pink wrap top and with a few wisps of hair around her face.

She sips from her wine and makes polite conversation with Dawn but I can kind of feel this silent battle going on in the air and I reckon that Mum is winning hands down because she's got this amused glint in her eye. Her voice is low and sophisticated when she asks questions and I'm not surprised when Dawn stands up, tugs at her short skirt as if to try and make it longer and thanks my parents for the wine.

'I'd better be off,' she says. 'I'm on duty first thing in the morning!'

She backs towards our front door under Mum's stare.

Mum makes no effort whatsoever to get up, so Dad goes to see Dawn out and I hear him murmur something under his breath but I can't catch what he's saying and all I see is Dawn colour a little and then make a hasty exit.

We hear the sound of the main door to the manor being locked, the sound of her heels clacking down the steps outside and an engine starting.

Then Mum stands up and claps her hands. Her face is a bit too flushed from the wine and something else – anger? Victory? I can't tell.

'I reckon we'll have a takeaway tonight,' she says. 'I fancy a night off cooking. Might go and do a bit of dancing downstairs.'

Then she floats out of the room leaving a cloud of Chanel perfume on the air behind her.

Dad and I gaze in the direction she's just gone in for a moment without speaking.

Then Dad breaks the trance by leaping up to grab his keys.

'Chinese?' he says. 'I won't be long.'

Then he slams out of the flat, leaving Ben and me alone.

We look at one another without speaking.

Ben slinks off to follow Mum down to the basement.

I go upstairs to my bedroom and curl up under the duvet for a bit.

Dad takes nearly an hour getting the food. He comes back in rubbing his hands and carrying two large bags with steaming hot Chinese food in them.

'Go get your mother,' he says to me.

I roll my eyes and swing my legs off the sofa where I'm now watching a re-run of *Gossip Girl*.

Dad starts opening boxes and packets and a gorgeous smell fills the air so I head off towards the basement to get Mum so that I can stuff my face as soon as possible.

On the way down to Mum's dance room I meet Ben sitting on the basement steps watching her through the window in the door.

'What are you doing?' I say. Stupid question, really. He's doing what he always does — hanging around and getting in the way.

I step over him and continue downstairs.

Mum is dancing with one spotlight trained down on to her so that she stands in a pool of light. She's standing on pointe, on one leg with the other stretched up high behind her.

I'm about to tell her that supper's ready but something stops me.

It's the look on her face.

It's like she's suddenly got five years younger or something. All the fine lines on her face have vanished and her skin is glowing. She's looking downwards at the floor and smiling like she's remembering something lovely that has happened.

I try to think when I last saw Mum's face looking like this but I can't. Suppose it's probably how she looked on stage most nights at the Royal Ballet when she curtseyed and took her bow whilst the audience threw red roses at her.

It's a beautiful look. Kind of pure and shining and glowing with love.

Maybe the fact that she got dressed up when Dawn came has made her feel better.

Anyway, it's kind of nice that she's looking so serene and not grey in the face with her usual migraine.

'Mum,' I say, then again, louder, 'MUM. Dinner is ready.'

My mother jumps and clutches her heart.

'Tabs, don't creep up on me like that,' she says, but she's still smiling.

By the time we get back upstairs to the kitchen her face has taken on its usual mask again and looks dull and cold.

I crunch my way through a bag of prawn crackers and text Gemma who now wants to come and spend a night in the manor because her parents reckon it's haunted.

'Don't bother,' I say. 'Nothing much ever

happens here.'

Then I wonder why I wrote that.

We go to bed early because Mum has faded back into tiredness again and Dad's going out to patrol once around the manor with Sid to check everything is OK.

I make sure that Ben is tucked up in the little room next to my own and then I lie in bed and try again to remember when it was that I last saw Mum's face looking so amazing.

I think and think and then at last, just as I'm dropping off, I see it.

It was the night Ben was born. He came at home because there was no time to get to the hospital and, after the midwife had left, Mum got up, clutching her sides and her back, and went over to the cot next to her bed.

She leant over the side of the cot and looked down at Ben.

Her face was all glowing with happiness.

She squeezed my hand and said, 'Look, Tabitha. Your new little brother. I hope you're going to take care of him.'

'Yeah,' I mutter to myself as I fall asleep. 'And I'm still taking care of him now.'

Then my eyelids slam down like steel shutters.

I dream of croquet all night long.

Chapter Seven

The next day Mum agrees that I can leave the flat.

I'm feeling loads better and I've almost managed to convince myself that everything weird I saw or felt in the manor was a dream connected to having the flu.

Every now and again there's this little voice in my head that whispers, 'But you KNOW it felt real,' and then I try hard to stamp it out again. I figure that if I fill my head with rubbish it will keep everything else at bay, so I watch loads of trashy telly, I sing loudly as I jump in the shower and I play CDs and text my mates and ring them on the phone to talk about nothing in particular – just school gossip and what Jake's up to now and whether I've done any of my half term homework yet (which I haven't, but I reckon that being ill is a good excuse).

I try to keep my head filled up with stuff and then I reckon that nothing else will be able to get in there.

'Coming with me around the manor?' Dad says after we've had cereal and coffee for breakfast. 'I've got to finish the upstairs inventory today.'

'I've got masses of homework,' I say. It's true enough, even though I don't much want to do it.

'Oh come on, Tabs,' says Dad. 'You'll love it.'

I freeze with my cup of coffee in my hand but Dad looks so big and reassuring and excited that I nod and try to look calm as I finish my breakfast.

So I can stick close to Dad, right? I don't need to go into any rooms on my own and even if I do I'm pretty sure that I was just feverish last time and imagining things.

The manor does look quite beautiful as we stroll down the long corridor from our flat to the entrance hall. It gleams in the sunlight and all the paintings are lit up, highlighting the beautiful faces of people who used to live here hundreds of years ago.

'Morning,' says Dad to Dawn as we pass the reception desk.

She flushes pink and busies herself with arranging a pile of guidebooks on the desk in front of her.

Visitors are already queuing up for tickets as we walk through the entrance hall.

I sneak a look at the fireplace but there's

nobody there, just an arrangement of dried orange flowers in the centre and, above it, the portrait of Lady Eleanor Thomas-Fulford in her long dark dress, her serious face in profile and a small black dog nestling at her feet.

'Miserable-looking woman, isn't she?' says Dad as he catches me looking. 'She loved this place, mind you. She refused to die until she'd made sure it would be left as a museum.'

We go into Lady Eleanor's morning room just as he's saying this and I catch my breath.

Lavender.

It's a choking smell.

I cough and pull my T-shirt up over my nose.

'What's wrong with you?' says Dad, amused. 'It's not dusty in here! Everything is cleaned, top to bottom.'

'No,' I say, struggling for breath. 'Can't you smell lavender, Dad?'

Dad takes a few deep sniffs.

'Nope,' he says. 'Faint smell of furniture polish.'

Maybe that's it. I'm glad when we've passed out of this room and gone up the ornate staircase but I keep a nervous eye on the door to the library.

Don't much fancy going in there after what happened last time.

'I need to do Mr Thomas-Fulford's bedroom today,' says Dad, and to my relief he takes me into a room I've not yet been into.

There's another of the ornate four-poster beds in the centre of the room but this one is made of brass and has a cream-coloured embroidered spread over the top.

There's a small round mirror with a three-tiered table underneath it by the window.

'Shaving mirror,' says Dad, ticking it off on his list. 'Shaving was a big thing for Victorian men. A manservant would have done it and it took ages.'

I nod and look around me. At the top of the bed are two long ropes hanging down, one on either side. There's a label on one of them which says 'Upstairs', and another one which says 'Servants' Hall'.

'Wow,' I say. 'So he could lie in bed and pull these and the servants would come up?'

'Not only that,' replies Dad, picking up a silver comb and inspecting it. 'You see that lever next to the ropes?'

I hadn't noticed it but there's a little handle on the wall and it's attached to a long gold pipe which runs right along the wall and ends up by the bedroom door on the other side of the room.

'Look,' says Dad. He pulls the handle and a bolt slams down into the lock on the bedroom door. 'So he didn't even have to get out of bed to lock his door. Clever stuff, eh?'

I nod, grinning. This house is full of surprises. Not all of them good, but this lever and lock thing is really brilliant, so I have a couple of goes of it myself and the rest of the morning passes smoothly. After lunch in the flat, I continue to go round the house with Dad and it's all light and cheerful in the two bedrooms he's working in so I feel OK, although I try not to look outside at the croquet lawn too much. When I do, all I can see is a group from the Women's Institute having a picnic underneath a tree and a coach-load of kids about to come into the manor to dress up as Victorian children and do loads of projects around the house.

It's kind of comforting seeing all this normal life going on and I feel better by the end of the day.

Then I get a text from Jake. It buzzes in my

pocket while I'm helping Dad inspect and check a soldier's uniform of a red-buttoned jacket and white trousers hanging in a glass-fronted cabinet in the guest bedroom.

'Hope you're having a cool half term,' it says. 'Worried about you. Haven't heard from you for ages. Do you want to meet up? J.'

'Ages' is in fact one day.

I put the phone back in my pocket without replying.

It's good helping Dad. The afternoon sun is streaming into the rooms and there's a nice feel up here, and Dad's good humour is infectious.

I help him polish some fenders and move furniture around, and then Dad and I head back to the flat feeling happy with our work.

Dawn's packing up and the last visitors have gone.

As we walk past her I try and will Dad not

to look at her but he's behind me and I can't quite see what he's doing, except he does linger for a moment by the reception desk. When I turn round Dawn pretends not to see me, reaches for her coat and heads off outside to her car.

Dad clears his throat and then bounds ahead of me to open up the flat.

'It's good living here, isn't it?' he says as we go in.

I smile but I don't say anything because it might not be what he wants to hear.

I mean – I enjoyed today with Dad. And the house is beautiful in the sunlight and it's kind of interesting looking at all the old things.

But – I can't shake the feeling that somebody or something is waiting in store for me and that I'm needed for something.

'Stupid,' I say to myself as I go into the warm flat.

Then Ben's hugging my knees and all my fears get forgotten in the chaos of him, asking what's for supper and Mum nagging me at least to try and do a bit of homework ready for Monday. I don't think much more about the manor.

Until.

Dad's cooking so he gets out one of his famous recipe books and then pats his pockets with a quizzical look on his broad face and he turns to me where I'm painting my fingernails a deep dark black. He says: 'Tabs, I think I've left my specs upstairs in Charles Thomas-Fulford's bedroom. Be a love and run up and get them. Here.'

He detaches a single key from the large group that always jangles from his hip and turns back to the fridge.

'Can't you go?' I say. My heart feels like it's going to stop.

'I'm cooking!' says Dad. 'Go on – you know where it is. Just make sure you lock up afterwards.'

I look at Mum. 'Will you come with me?' I say. 'Please?'

Mum laughs. 'Don't be silly. And anyway, I don't really like the place at night. Too many shadows.'

Oh great.

So she's scared of the manor but it's OK to send me up there in the dark.

'You won't be in the dark,' says Dad, reading my mind. 'It's not dark outside yet. If you need to switch on a light, you know where they are. OK?'

I'm running out of excuses now so I get up, put my phone in my pocket and slide my feet back into my flip-flops.

'If I'm not back in five minutes will you come and get me?' I whine as I leave.

Dad gives me an exasperated look from where he's chopping onions so I head into the corridor outside our flat.

The door clangs shut behind me and for a moment I consider letting myself back in and pleading cowardice.

But Dad will go mad. He hates me acting up and stressing out Mum.

I take a deep breath.

'It's all fine,' I say to myself as I walk along the corridor past the dining room and drawing room. The doors are shut and locked so at least I won't be able to look inside.

I reach the entrance hall. The desk looks bare without all the postcards and books laid out and there's a smell of polish and beeswax because the cleaners have been in today.

'Just go straight upstairs,' I say to myself, gripping the large key Dad's given me. 'Upstairs and across the landing and into that room, grab the glasses and get back to the flat. OK?'

I wonder why I appear to be having a conversation with myself, but it kind of works because I find myself at the foot of the stairs about to go up.

I stand by the arched cabinet that used to be a doorway and part of me registers that it's really quite cold where I'm standing.

And then I freeze for real.

The staircase is twisted so that I can only see the bit that goes up straight ahead of me and then there's a small landing in the middle and a further few stairs which are over my head but which I can't see from where I'm standing.

Except that I can hear them.

Somebody's footsteps.

Coming downstairs.

Heavy, slow, like an old person or an

overweight person or somebody who needs to take their time coming down.

I stand rooted to the spot with my eyes growing wider and my heart pounding and my hand closing over the mobile to call Dad except I'm too scared to make a sound so I just carry on standing there.

The steps continue to come down, one at a time and then when they reach the landing and I'm feeling like my heart's going to burst . . . they stop.

A dark shadow passes over the oak-panelled wall and fades away.

Then nothing.

I can't move. It's like somebody has got a giant glue gun and glued my feet to the tiled floor.

Around me the house seems to take a deep sigh. I swear I feel the walls around me shudder.

It's dead quiet.

I listen for the sound of the grandfather clock on the staircase but I can't hear it. I strain for the clank of the central heating pipes or the quiet beep of the movement sensors on the ceiling.

Nothing.

I look up at one of the security cameras above my head. It's pointing straight at me and I get the weirdest feeling. It's like Sid is on the desk and watching me on his computer screen. Except there's nobody on reception at this time of night.

So who's watching me?

The camera gives a little jerk and starts to move back and forth like it's shaking its head at me.

The spell of silence is broken.

I realise that where I'm standing is so cold that my bones are aching and I find my legs again and run back towards the flat at top speed with my flip-flops slapping on the parquet entrance hall floor.

I don't stop to look at anything and I avoid looking at the dining-room door by turning my head the other way. I just run and focus on the brown door of our flat until I'm right beside it.

My hands are shaking so hard that I can't put my key in the lock so I just bang and bang on the door until Mum opens it with a scared look on her face and I rush into her arms.

And that's where I stay.

Dad doesn't believe a word of it.

He's annoyed because he has to go upstairs in the manor and get his glasses back, leaving onions simmering and Mum under strict instructions not to burn them.

'You are silly, Tabs,' he says when he gets back. 'Honestly! There's nobody there on the stairs and it's not even all that cold. I don't know where you get your sensitive nature from.'

He glances at Mum when he says this and she glares back.

'I don't care what you think,' I murmur from inside Mum's fleece where I'm hiding my head. Mum strokes my hair like when I was little, and Ben sits on my lap and plays with my earrings. 'I heard footsteps and that's that.'

Dad serves up his dinner masterpiece and it tastes good but my appetite has totally vanished and I feel sick and shaky.

'Can I sleep in your room tonight?' I say to Mum and she sighs, but nods her head, so I put my blue sleeping bag on the floor and listen to Dad snoring and Mum breathing all night. At one point I wake up and swear that she's crying, and another time I wake up and she doesn't even seem to be there and I almost think that I hear her talking in Ben's room which is a bit weird at that time of night but I'm so tired that I go right back to sleep again and when I wake up in the morning it's Friday and she's already gone down to the basement to practise.

Dad's gone into town to do a food shop and Ben's curled up watching children's television. There's no way on this earth that I'm going to leave the flat and enter the manor, even though it's filled with visitors, so I sit up in my bedroom and try to read a book but my heart's not really in it.

Then there's a pounding on the door and I freeze yet again and sit cross-legged on my bed wondering what to do. There's another loud knock and I figure that it could be an emergency and that Dad would want me to answer it so I creep downstairs to the door and say in a shaky voice, 'Yes. Hello. Who is it?' The booming voice of Sid answers so I undo the lock and let him in, my face flooded red with relief and embarrassment.

'Your dad in?' says Sid. He's so big that he fills the entire door frame in his white security-guard shirt and dark trousers with the mobile walkie-talkie attached next to a bunch of keys.

'Sorry,' I reply. 'He's gone into town to buy food. Do you want to wait? He won't be long.'

Sid glances back to the entrance hall and then gives me his broad grin. 'If you throw a cup of tea into the bargain, I reckon I will,' he says.

He sits down next to Ben on the sofa and Ben, after giving him a scared look, decides that Sid isn't a threat and so sticks his thumb in his mouth and continues to watch *Shaun the Sheep* without further communication.

'Ah,' says Sid, downing tea like he's the thirstiest man in Britain. 'That's nice, pet. Thanks.'

I smile. Sid's got this broad Geordie accent. It kind of goes with his big body and shiny bald head.

'You settling in, lass?' he enquires, leaning back on the sofa and giving me a long stare. 'Bit of an acquired taste here, isn't it?'

I'm not quite sure what he means by this so I offer him another Rich Tea biscuit. He takes three and dunks them into his teacup in the way that Mum always tells me not to.

'Why do the security cameras move about at night?' I say. I've never managed to quite work out what was going on with the cameras.

Sid pauses a moment to scoop some Rich Tea out of his mug with a teaspoon.

'They're not supposed to,' he says. 'All the outside doors are alarmed at night and that's how we stop intruders getting in. I probably left the computer on by mistake.'

I hate it when grown-ups don't tell you the

truth. I know full well that the computer wasn't even on at the reception desk when I passed by last night. But Sid's nice and I don't want to make him feel awkward so I leave the subject and we talk about Mum's dancing and Sid tells me he's been working at the manor for nearly fifteen years now, and then, as Dad still isn't back, he decides he'd better get back to work.

There's a crackle on his radio so he responds and is about to leave the flat when I find this voice I didn't know I had and I say: 'Wait. Have you ever heard anything weird here? Like – footsteps. Or have you ever seen any ladies?'

I go bright red after saying this but Sid doesn't laugh, like Dad, or shudder, like Mum, or tell me to stop being daft.

He just gives me this matter-of-fact look and speaks into his radio, telling Dawn he'll be back in a moment to take a crowd of visitors down to the basement kitchens and might they do the upstairs attics while they're waiting.

Then he comes back in and sits down on the sofa again.

'Aye,' he says. 'Happen I have. Seen something, I mean. It was a while ago now.'

Although I've gone all shivery and I don't really want to hear what he's about to say, another smaller part of me is really desperate to hear more so I nod but don't say anything.

'It was when I came in early one morning to unlock,' he says. 'Quite unexpected, it was. One minute nobody there. The next she was there in front of me.'

The radio crackles into life again. Dawn sounds like she's going to blow a fuse. Sid gets up, wipes his brow with a big white handkerchief and gives me a wink.

'We know who wears the trousers around here,' he says.

He pats me on the head like I'm about three and I don't mind because it's so good to know that I'm not actually going barking bonkers. 'We'll talk again,' he says. 'I might be able to explain some stuff about the house if you're interested.'

'Yeah,' I say. 'Yeah, I am.'

I'm frightened to death as well, but I don't need to tell him cos I reckon he can see that.

'Thanks for the tea,' says Sid. 'I'd better be off now.'

I don't know what makes me do it, but I reach up and plant a big kiss on his shiny cheek.

'Ah, bless you, lass,' he says. 'Tell your dad I'm looking for him.'

He disappears off down the corridor, jingling the bunch of keys.

Chapter Eight

The next day Dad bounds into the flat with something clasped behind his back.

'This should cheer you up, Tabs,' he says, coming over to where I'm lying on my stomach with my legs up in the air, texting Gemma. 'Here – give me that.'

He ignores my squawk of protest and whips my mobile phone off me.

'Dad!' I say. 'I need my mobile like ALL the time! What if somebody texts me?'

'I'm sure you'll survive five minutes without it,' says Dad. He slips my mobile phone into the pocket of his jeans and then instructs me to close my eyes.

I'm not too keen on doing that at the moment. Every time I close my eyes at night I see a white moony face and hear the heavy thump of footsteps descending the manor staircase.

'Go on,' says Dad. 'Just for a moment.'

I half-close my eyes so that I can still see a blurry outline of Dad's face. He puts something cold, small and smooth into my hands and I open my eyes right away and gasp.

'Dad!' I say. 'I've always wanted one of these!'

I slide my fingers over the tiny flat screen and it beeps into life.

Dad has bought me an iPhone. It's black and shiny and new. And perfect.

'Thanks,' I say, leaping up to throw my arms round his neck.

'Hmm,' mutters Mum who is mixing up a bowl of cereal and prunes behind me. She says

119

it helps her stomach but I can't see how. It looks disgusting. I've got a pile of toast and Marmite next to me. 'That must have cost a lot of money. I hope you're going to look after it, Tabitha.'

I pull a face at Dad and he sparkles back at me.

'Got it off Kevin cheap,' he says. 'He's put some stuff on it for you, Tabs. Not sure what.'

Kevin is Dad's best friend from college. They've always kept in touch. Nobody's quite sure what Kevin does for a living but he's always got loads of electrical equipment to sell and half our flat is furnished with it.

Mum sniffs.

'Knock-off,' she says. 'That's nice. Great example you're setting our daughter.'

Dad pulls a face behind her back and I smother a grin.

Then Mum slopes back off to her bedroom to eat the muesli, and I spend the rest of the morning fiddling about with my new toy and emailing Gemma.

Dad's helping Mum paint the bathroom this morning but when he's done a couple of hours he leaves her to it and prepares to go and carry out some jobs in the manor.

'There was a reason I bought you the iPhone,' he says as he passes the sofa. 'I thought perhaps you could take some photographs for me of each of the rooms? I need a rough picture of all the contents to back up my inventory.'

I freeze.

'Today?' I say. 'Do I have to do it today?'

Dad ruffles my hair.

'Well as you're about to go back to school, this is kind of the last chance, isn't it?' he says. 'I'll be around the house if you need me.

It won't take you all that long.'

I sigh. My appetite has shrivelled away to nothing.

'Can I ask Gem to come over and help me?' I say.

Dad's smile fades a little.

'Really, Tabs,' he says. 'What's up with you? You used to be such a strong girl. But yes – if you like. Invite Gemma. I'm sure your mum will give her lunch.'

He goes out into the corridor and shuts the flat door behind him.

I sit there for a moment trying not to be upset by what he said.

Thing is – Dad's right. I did use to be strong. I used to be brave and funny and would do anything that anybody asked me.

I shiver and text Gem from my new iPhone and she texts back right away that she'd love to come over and I smile and think, *If Gemma is here then nothing will happen. Things will be OK.*

Gem comes in all brown and glowing from the sun and wearing a white strappy sun dress and flip-flops.

I see her look for a moment at my faded jeans and unwashed hair but she's a good mate and says nothing.

I know I look a bit rubbish at the moment. I haven't slept very well either so I have circles the colour of purple cabbage underneath my eyes and I've lost weight, so my jeans are held up by a belt so they don't end up down by my feet.

'You OK, Tabs?' is all she says. I nod. She reaches out and gives me a gentle hug. She's good like that, Gem. She knows when something is going on but she's never pushy.

The thing about telling stuff to your best mate is that it kind of makes it REAL. Maybe if I just don't admit to anything it will kind of go away and leave me alone.

Gemma loves coming into the manor. She twirls down the corridor past the vast dining room, getting looks of disapproval from a group of Japanese visitors who are clustered in front of the Chinese lions and then she does a little tap dance in the entrance hall on the parquet floor.

Dawn laughs when she sees this.

'I'll have some of whatever your friend is on, Tabs,' she says as I run behind to catch up.

Gem has spun off into the large drawing room and is staring up at the crystal chandelier and at the gilt mirrors placed at either end of the room over the ornate fireplaces.

'They must have had some cool parties in here,' she says.

I smile.

'Oh, we still do!' says Gemma in a posh voice.

Huh?

I turn to Gemma. 'What do you mean? Why did you say that?'

Gemma frowns. 'I didn't say anything, or I don't think I did, anyway.'

It's my turn to frown, but Gemma has turned away and is gazing out through the French double doors at the back lawn of the manor. There are groups of kids lounging about all over it, lying in the sun, listening to radios or fiddling with their phones.

'You're so lucky living here,' she says. 'My mum's flat is so boring. And we haven't even got a garden.'

Seeing the kids with their phones reminds me that I'm supposed to be on a mission for Dad, so I get out my new iPhone and let

Gem play about with it for a bit and then I find the camera application and take a wonky photograph of the blue and green Wedgwood in its case near the door.

We study the results.

'Bit blurry,' says Gem. 'But not bad for an amateur.'

I roll my eyes at her and then we go into the dining room and I take another photograph, this time of the Chinese lions and the photo's better, with sunshine glinting off their fierce faces and I feel almost cheerful because at last I'm having fun and being useful and for a change – I'm not feeling scared.

'Let's do upstairs,' Gemma says. 'I like those grand bedrooms.'

It's a bit like the sun goes in when she says this but I've got a job to do for Dad and I've got Gemma right here next to me, so I smile and we head up the brown staircase without me pausing to think about the footsteps I heard. I take a series of shots of Lady Eleanor's bed with the floral bedspread and her dressing table with the silver-backed brushes and I'm really getting into this now so I carry on, going from room to room and clicking away on my new gadget. When we've done all the first-floor rooms we head downstairs and then Gemma stops at the bottom of the stairs and says, 'Take a picture of the staircase, Tabs – your dad will want a record of all these paintings.' She's right, so we stand at the bottom of the staircase and I take a couple of quick photographs before Gemma gets really hungry and we head back to the flat to see if Mum has got lunch.

I kind of remember this morning for a long time afterwards.

For three hours, I wasn't scared.

For three hours, I had fun.

For three hours, I managed to stop being Tabitha Grey the weirdo and just be 'Tabs' the teenage girl, on half term and having a good time with her best mate.

Three hours is not very long, really.

Mum cooks us up a pasta thing with bits of bacon in it and Gem devours the whole plateful like it's the last meal she's ever going to eat or something, and I pick at mine and try to look like I'm enjoying it.

'Are you still feeling off-colour?' asks Mum, placing her hand on my forehead. 'You do look a bit peaky. You're not hot, though – cold, if anything.'

I sigh.

'Don't worry,' I say. 'I'm OK. I've probably just got a summer cold or something.'

Mum looks doubtful but pulls a tub of chocolate-chip ice cream out of the freezer, gives me and Gem a spoon each and leaves us to it.

Then I try to link up my new iPhone to my laptop and Gemma helps me. It doesn't actually take very long at all and there are all my colour photographs downloading on to the screen so that I can look at them blown up in size and decide which ones I'm going to email to Dad for his inventory.

'They're good,' says Gem. She's curled up in the corner of the sofa next to Ben and he's got his head on her shoulder. Ben always did like Gem. She's fun and soft-hearted, just the sort of person he likes. He stares up at her with his thumb stuck in his mouth and she fiddles with her jewellery and her phone and asks me embarrassing questions about Jake, and then her phone rings and it's her mum asking her to come home and pick up some food shopping on the way. So she goes at three o'clock. Mum has gone for a lie-down so it's just me and Ben and the photographs.

I page through the photos and admire my handiwork.

'I could make a career out of this!' I say to Ben, but he's not very interested in my mad plans for the future and sits on the floor instead, so I page through on my own.

'That's good,' I say, when the picture of the Chinese lions comes up. 'Dad could use that.'

I run through all the photographs until I reach the very last one.

'Oh,' I say. It's the one I took on the staircase and there's a dark smudge right in the middle of the photo which I stupidly rub on the screen.

I hit the zoom button and the photo on the staircase is blown up to about five times the original size.

For a moment I can't think what I am looking at. And then I look a little closer, and as I stare I feel my skin going clammy and my hands turning ice-cold.

It's not a smudge.

The more I stare at it, the more I see.

There's the outline of a black dress. Long, with a nipped-in waist and a corset top.

No head.

There's an arm, though.

A white arm, reaching out to touch the carved oak banisters of the manor staircase.

And at the very bottom of the black smudge, a smaller shape with fuzzy edges so that I have to stare and stare even though I really don't want to and my ears are buzzing like a faulty fridge.

I know what it is even before I work out the shape.

It's tiny, black and with pointy ears.

One of Lady Eleanor's dogs.

On the floor next to me, Ben starts to cry.

When Dad comes back into our flat I'm huddled in the corner of the sofa with my laptop still on.

I've got to show Dad and he's got to see it. He's got to start believing me. He's got to. Otherwise I might go mad soon. Either that or I will just drop dead of being scared.

'Good day?' says Dad, filling the kettle behind me and then coming to see what I'm doing.

Honestly. He must be one of the most unobservant people on the planet. I mean – you'd only have to look at my pale face and runny eyeliner to know that I'd been crying. But Dad seems never to see things like that. He doesn't see it in Mum, either. Sometimes he thinks she's been having a great time when really she's been crying herself to sleep and refusing to eat.

Dad flings himself down next to me and loosens his top shirt button.

'Hey, you've done the photos!' he says. 'Mind if I have a look?'

He pages through the pictures making the odd comment and then he gets to the last one.

'Oh, shame about the blurry bit,' he says. 'Never mind. You can do it again another time for me.'

I don't say anything. I lean forwards and click the magnify button so that Dad is looking at exactly the same thing I've just had to see.

He peers a bit more closely. Then he gets his glasses out and puts them on the end of his nose and peers again.

I watch his face.

It goes from being puzzled to being something else. Just for a split second. For an instant my dad looks unsettled. Like somebody took the wind out of his sails. Then a great big smile breaks over his face.

'Nice one, Tabs!' he says. 'You nearly had me going there! I didn't realise that Kevin had put that app on for you. Well, it obviously works!'

I feel my heart sinking towards my feet.

'What app?' I say.

'The Photoshop app!' says Dad. 'You've worked out how to use it already. I'm impressed!'

I shake my head so hard that I give myself a headache.

'No, I don't know what you mean, Dad,' I say. 'I haven't got a Photoshop app. I don't even know what it is.'

Dad laughs and goes over to make himself a cup of tea.

'Kevin must have thought you'd enjoy it,'

he says. 'Downloaded it on to your phone as a surprise. Probably thought you could have some fun messing about with it. I mean – the manor's a brilliant place for doing fake photos, isn't it?

This is some kind of joke. Doesn't Dad realise that this sort of stuff isn't exactly my idea of fun?

'I don't even know how to find the app,' I whisper but Dad has already got tired of me and my photos and has gone off to have a shower, so I just put my arm around Ben and we sit there in silence for ages until Mum wakes up and comes out to make dinner.

She's in a good mood and I so want to tell her everything, but Mum's funny about hearing anything to do with ghosts and so I can't.

There's nobody I can turn to for help and nobody believes me.

Except Ben.

But he's too little to do anything about it.

I watch television with Mum while we're eating supper but I can't remember a thing about what we watched.

We have to carry on living here. And I'm more frightened than I've ever been in my life.

Chapter Nine

It's like this huge relief to get back to school for the rest of the term.

Never thought I'd hear myself think that, but it's true.

I even want to see Jake now. We never got to meet up in the end what with me being ill or him playing football and now I want to see somebody ordinary and do normal boyfriend/girlfriend stuff like going shopping and seeing films.

After a really bad night's sleep I can hardly wait to run down the corridor to the front door of Weston Manor and burst out into the fresh air.

Not sure I ever want to come back.

I leave Mum and Dad arguing in the kitchen. I can't quite make out what it's about because they're conducting the entire row in muttered voices under their breath so that I can't hear, but I catch Ben's name and my own and Mum is pale with black circles under her eyes, which means that the migraines have come back.

As I leave the flat I swear I hear Mum mention Dawn, but I'm not sure.

She hasn't arrived yet. It's too early for her to be setting up her desk. There's a cleaner polishing windows in the entrance hall and a man up a ladder fixing a light bulb but other than that the manor feels kind of empty and calm.

Not like it did the other day when I heard the steps on the stairs.

'Weird old house,' I mutter as I heave open the enormous front door. The cleaner hears me and thinks I'm speaking to her so I have to spend another five minutes making polite conversation with the old lady in an apron holding a plastic bucket.

'Expect you'll be looking forward to this evening,' she says.

I'm halfway out of the door but I turn around, sneaking a quick look at my watch. The bus will be outside the manor in one and a half minutes and I'm going to have to run like stink to make it.

'This evening?' I say. 'Why? What's happening?'

The woman laughs, snapping off her rubber gloves and rolling them into a ball.

'Can't believe that your father hasn't told you,' she says. 'We have a ghost hunt on the second Monday evening of every month.

People pay a lot of money to get a look around this house at night-time.'

I fight an urge to burst out in uncontrollable fits of giggles.

There's not much point me telling her that all the action I've witnessed so far has taken place in the DAY.

But then it's like she reads my mind and she says: 'Most people don't see anything. Mind, there's been one or two who can.'

That's got my interest. I can hear in the distance the sound of the bus engine whining by but I don't care.

'Who?' I say. 'Sid?'

The cleaner laughs again.

'He wouldn't let on if he had,' she says. 'But some of the volunteers and guides who work here have had something happen to them. Doors slamming, voices. That kind of thing.'

I laugh in what's supposed to be a scornful way.

'But those things could be caused by real-life people,' I say. 'How do you know it's anything to do with ghosts?'

The woman leans her mop against the reception desk and gives me a considered look.

'I don't believe in it, myself,' she says. 'Nothing's ever happened to me.'

I notice she's wearing a tiny gold cross around her neck. When she says this, it glints and sparkles in the sunlight coming through the windows.

Then she turns away, shaking her head and smiling an annoying little smirk so I pelt down the steps and out across the gravel drive towards the entrance gates with their carved pineapples on top. I wait for the next bus and spend the rest of the morning explaining to teachers why I was too late to make assembly.

Jake comes up to me during break-time. Tie too short. Shirt un-tucked and crinkled. Trousers baggy and falling down around his skinny hips.

Not fair. If I even so much as wear an ear hoop the teachers are down on me like a ton of bricks and all of the girls have to wear their hair in ponytails or hair-bands during the day. My hair's too fine to be worn in either of those ways but there's no point arguing with the teachers or you just get shoved into detention after school.

So I'm just sitting on a wall banging my heels against the brick and watching a couple of girls try to scratch each other's eyes out when Jake comes up to me all casual and says, 'Awight?'

'Yeah,' I say. 'At least, I think so. There's some weird stuff going on at home but apart from that.'

'Yeah?' says Jake, but I can tell that he's not interested in what's going on at the manor. He's looking me up and down and hopping from leg to leg.

'So,' I say, trying to get his attention back. 'Good half term?'

Jake lets his dark blue eyes rest on me for a moment.

'It was OK,' he says. 'Sorry we never got to meet up in the end though. I kind of, erm, like, missed you.'

Then he goes all red and turns away to fake interest in what's going on in the football field.

I smile. I've decided to be nicer to Jake. It's good to hear that somebody likes me.

The bell rings for afternoon double maths. I groan and get up.

'Don't s'pose you fancy doing something later?' says Jake, staring at the ground and kicking the gravel into dust. 'Film or something?'

'OK,' I say. 'I'll have to ring Mum but say I'll see you outside school at four?'

Jake nods and slopes off for an afternoon of chemistry.

I head into maths feeling like it's my birthday and Valentine's Day all rolled into one.

A night off from the manor! I can't wait.

Mum's a bit edgy when I call her just before four and explain that I'm going out for a couple of hours with Jake.

'It's not that I don't trust you,' she says. 'Or Jake. It's just – well, you know what it is.'

I do know, but I don't want to bring the subject up on the phone so I just say, 'I know, yes, but I'm nearly fifteen and we've been going out over five months and I'll be fine and I'll see you just after supper. OK?'

Mum agrees. I can hear the anxiety in her voice. She's been given new pills by the doctors, which are supposed to stop the worry, but some days it seems as if they're not really working.

I hang up and shake my fair hair out of the horrid ponytail just in time for Jake to come strolling out of the school and in my direction.

We go to the precinct and Jake pays for us to see a film in 3D which is kind of cool and although it's a stupid film I really enjoy having one night where I don't have to worry about weird atmospheres and strange noises.

I let Jake put his arm round me in the film.

I feel kind of safe and warm.

Afterwards we go to Pizza Express and I wolf down a Four Seasons. When I eventually look at my watch and realise I ought to be getting back to Mum and Dad, it's like somebody has poured a bucket of cold black water over my head and all the happy feelings start to snake their way out of the building to be replaced by little thrills of fear and nerves.

'Let's walk back,' says Jake.

We walk down the long main road towards the manor and just as we turn the corner and it comes into sight he slips his hand into mine but, although I've got used to it, by then I can see the large square whiteness of the house with its green shutters and great expanse of parkland and I'm feeling like I want to ask Jake's parents to adopt me quick.

'Funny place you live in,' says Jake as we reach the huge gates. 'Kind of like some posh person's house from the last century.'

'Well, that's what it is,' I say. 'Five centuries, in fact. The last family to live here owned it for over a hundred years.'

I'm sounding a bit like Dad on one of his research highs so I stop quick and let Jake peck me on the cheek. His mouth is warm and smells of popcorn.

'Look after yourself, yeah?' he says.

His voice is more serious than usual and his eyes look dark and concerned. Maybe he's noticed that I'm not really quite with it at the moment.

I watch as he turns away and lopes off down Weston Drove.

Then I trail up the enormous semi-circular drive and ring the bell of Weston Manor.

Dad is really in his element tonight.

There are two big groups of adults going round the house for the ghost hunts and Dad's job as Keeper is to welcome them and give them some history of the house and its occupants before passing them over to the two female guides who will take the groups around the big state rooms, up to the bedrooms and then down to the basement kitchens.

The guides are both wearing fancy dress. Just looking at them makes me want to giggle.

One of them, a fair-haired lady with a pretty, round face, is dressed a bit like a giant white fairy in a glittery white dress with wings attached to the back. The other has dressed like a cross between a Victorian servant and a mad witch, all in black with a pointy hat, long black skirts and buttoned-up high boots with stripy socks.

'Nice that they make the effort, isn't it?' says Dad as he clears his throat and shuffles his notes ready to welcome the visitors to Weston. 'Do you want to go round with one of the groups, Tabs? You're almost an adult.'

I shudder. Just the thought of going upstairs again, even in a big group of people, doesn't appeal very much.

'No, I think I'll go back to the flat and see Mum,' I say. 'Tired, you know.'

I'm still feeling happy after my evening with Jake but Dad doesn't need to know all that.

'Well in that case, could you show Mrs Spencer to the ladies' loo on the way?' says Dad. I sigh but smile at Mrs Spencer and take her out of the entrance hall through a door to the left and into the public toilets.

As she disappears into a cubicle, I glance around the room and wonder what it used to be. There's a huge white arched door on one side of it, blocked in now. Maybe it's always been a loo. Or maybe it was a room for the butler to clean silver in? It's cold, in any case, and the black-and-white tiled floor makes me feel dizzy if I look at it too long.

I'm standing looking in the mirror at myself and listening to Dad's voice booming out from the morning room and wondering if I should chop my hair short, and Mrs Spencer is rustling about and flushing in her cubicle and then I feel a slight tickle on my neck, like somebody has just touched it very gently and there's a sudden strong scent of soap or washing powder. I'm staring in the mirror trying to see what it is when Mrs Spencer comes out of the cubicle and says, 'Spider alert! You've got an enormous one on your neck.'

'Yes, I know,' I snap. In fact I didn't, but I hate spiders.

'I've got it,' she says, brushing the back of my neck with a sharp movement. 'That was huge! Must have fallen from the ceiling on to your hair.'

She bustles off back to the ghost hunt without needing my help any longer. I can still hear Dad talking in his big booming Keeper's voice.

The smell of soap has vanished.

I stare at the floor.

The spider sits where it fell and then it scuttles off towards the big arched door.

It's minute. Tiny. If I'd seen it on myself I

wouldn't have freaked at all. Mrs Spencer must have an eyesight problem.

'Strange,' I say but everyone's gone so I go back towards our flat to see Mum, and, as I walk down the corridor past the grand dining room, somebody rushes out from the darkness within and brushes past me so fast that I can't see who it is. So I turn around and stare behind me and all I see is part of a blue dress whisking round the corner back into the entrance hall.

I stand for a moment, my head in a whirl.

In the background I can hear the comforting boom of Dad's voice and the laughter of the people on the ghost tour. 'She must have been late for the tour,' I say to myself. Somehow it seems important to say this. 'Visitors are often late.'

Then I turn the key into our flat and slam the door behind me.

It's dark inside so I call out, 'Mum?' and

then I realise she's watching TV in the lounge in the dark.

She jumps about a mile high when I poke my head round the door.

'Tabitha, you gave me a fright!' she says, shifting along the sofa to make room for me. 'Did you have a nice time with Jake?'

I nod but I'm too embarrassed to go into details.

'What are you watching?' I say. The television is jumping about in strange zigzags and two scared-looking presenters are being filmed with night-vision cameras.

'Silly rubbish,' says Mum. 'It's this programme where two people go into haunted houses and try to film ghosts. Most of it's made up for the cameras but it's weirdly addictive when you get into it.'

I shudder and get up to make myself a hot chocolate.

When I come back Mum has fallen asleep with the remote in her hand so I click the television off and cover her with a blanket. Then I read in bed and wait for Dad to come in.

'It was brilliant,' he says when we're sitting in the lamplight at the kitchen table.

'Did you see anything?' I say, studying my feet in their pink slippers. I kind of know what his answer is going to be.

'No, not really,' says Dad. 'But they enjoyed looking round the rooms in the candlelight. One person reckoned that they'd heard a voice but nobody else heard it so it's a bit difficult to say.'

He yawns and drains his mug of coffee.

'Early start tomorrow,' he says. 'And you should have been in bed hours ago. It's only Monday. Don't want your schoolwork to start suffering.'

I groan. I'm about to head off to bed when I remember something. 'Dad,' I say. 'What about that woman in the blue dress? Did she enjoy it?'

Dad frowns and clicks off the kitchen light.

'I don't recall anyone wearing a blue dress. Most people were wearing jeans. But then again I couldn't see everything. It was pretty dark in most of the rooms. Night, Tabs.'

He leaves me sitting there in the dark.

A chill creeps up and starts to penetrate my heart.

Chapter Ten

There's not much point trying to convince Dad that I really did see somebody rush out of the dining room last night.

He just comes up with an irritating scientific explanation for everything, or else he tries to make out that my imagination is running away with me.

'Old houses have draughts, Tabs,' he says. 'You of all people should know that.'

I growl. It's the next day and I'm eating toast and cereal in the kitchen with Ben playing hide-and-seek under the table.

'Dad,' I say. 'I'm not mad. I saw her dress

as clearly as I'm seeing you now.'

Dad ruffles my hair in a really annoying way.

'Yeah, sure,' he says. 'We all know what you're like about seeing things, Tabs.'

Mum shoots him a look when he says this.

'Don't start that again,' she hisses. Her pale face is half-hidden under her wing of brown hair and she's wrapped up in a thick pink towelling dressing gown even though it's about ninety degrees outside.

Dad sighs, grabs a triangle of toast from my plate and gets himself ready for another day compiling his new brochure on the manor. He's got a photographer coming today to take glossy pictures and encourage even more visitors to pour through the heavy doors.

'Our brochure will be the best yet,' he says. 'You'll see.'

'Are you going to put in any photos of the

family who used to live here?' I say. 'That Lady Eleanor woman?'

Mum and Dad exchange another weird look. They do a lot of that lately.

I hate it.

'It's a fair question!' I say.

Dad grabs his jacket from a hook by the door and bolts off into the manor, leaving Mum to deal with me.

'You don't need to know everything all the time, Tabitha,' she says. 'And I don't want to hear any more from you. We've come here for a fresh start. Remember?'

Then she blows her nose and heads off towards the shower.

I can't concentrate at school.

OK, that's partly because Jake keeps looking over at me during assembly. I keep wondering if he's gone off me or if we'll go out again soon. I check my phone all day and there are no texts or anything, so my good mood deflates like a tyre and I land myself with yet another detention for not paying attention to the teacher in biology cos I'm half thinking about Jake and half thinking about the weird things that are going on at Weston Manor.

When the bell goes at the end of the school day I hang around the gates for a while just in case Jake's going to come out and walk me home, but I see him head off towards the sports field and I realise that it's the night when his class does extra football practice after school. I go back inside because I've got a half-four detention and I spend an hour copying out a chapter of my biology textbook under the watchful glare of Miss Mayfield and then she lets me go a bit early because we're both sweltering in the hot classroom. I get on the bus and sit in a warm fug of sweat and misery until it drops me off at end of the long road which runs parallel to the manor.

I walk up the front drive and stare up at the house.

It stares back, with its unblinking windows half-hidden behind green shutters.

There are loads of cars parked in the drive which means the manor is full of visitors.

The air is very warm out here but the thought of going inside makes me shiver, so instead I go through the arch on the left-hand side of the house and into the grounds at the back of the house.

The croquet hoops still sit in the grass but there's nobody there.

I study the hoops close-up but they just look like semi-circular bits of iron.

I glance up at the house and at the window to the library where I stood looking out on the day I saw the three women playing their game.

The curtains are drawn across the window. Dad sometimes does that to stop the sun streaming in and fading the valuable old books.

'It's a lovely house,' I say to myself out loud. 'You are lucky to live here. Get a grip, Tabs!' My voice sounds harsh in the silence.

It doesn't really sound like me.

I glance up towards the house again and then to my right. The tiny church of St Paul and Peter sits surrounded by bushes of pink and purple flowers. It looks kind of calm and safe so I walk away from the manor gardens and through the little gate that joins them to the churchyard.

It's peaceful in here, although the birds are chirping and there's the faint sound of organ music coming from inside the church. I pick my way through the gravestones, looking at some of the names, or at least the ones that aren't so faded with age that it's impossible to make out even the dates. Some of them are so old that they are angled outwards, like ancient grey teeth falling from a long-dead mouth. I shudder and walk into the church.

There's no organist there. This puzzles me for a bit but then I see that there's a tape playing. The tiny church is empty except for a lady in an apron who is filling up buckets and vases with sprays of white lilies.

'Hello,' she says. 'We've got a wedding in here on Saturday. Beautiful church, isn't it?'

I smile and start to walk around. I'm conscious that the lady is watching me over the top of her flowers. Suppose most teenage girls don't spend their after-school hours wandering around small local churches.

Then again, I'm not most teenage girls.

I walk down the aisle to look at the altar and then down one side of the church. The wall is covered with gold plaques and with a jolt I realise that they are all memorials to the Thomas-Fulford family.

There's one for Lady Eleanor and another for her husband, Sir Charles. Beneath that is a plaque with two names on – Lucinda and Rose MacDonald, Lady Eleanor's half-sisters. There are five plaques to earlier members of the family with dates stretching back over four hundred years. And then sticking out on its own next to a pillar is one for John Thomas-Fulford.

'Captain Jack,' I say out loud.

There's a loud cough behind me so I turn around expecting the flower lady to be there ready to boot me out, but she's still on the other side of the church arranging armfuls of leafy green ferns amidst the white flowers.

'OK,' I say to myself. 'Maybe I should get more sleep.'

This is my new way of dealing with things. I'm going to be like Dad and find a rational explanation for every single thing that happens to me from now on.

I say goodbye to the lady in the church and head back out into the graveyard.

It's boiling out here now.

When I went in the church it was warm, but now it feels more like the height of an August summer holiday than early June.

I take off my school tie and shove it into my bag, open a few buttons of my shirt at the neck and gulp down water from a bottle.

There's a buzzing in the air, like crickets or grasshoppers or something you'd hear in a film set in another, hotter country.

'Summer flies,' I say to myself. 'It might be flying ant day.'

I shudder. Dad says that flying ants only swarm on one day of the year and that they are all dead by the end of it. Can't really see the point of that myself.

I look for ants, but I can't see any.

There's a tiny path leading to the left so I walk down it only to come to a dead end blocked by a curved granite bench, so I come back and wander around the newer part of the graveyard on the other side of the church.

The stones here are grander, made out of blocks and spires of stone, some with crosses looming up high and others with angels standing in silent concrete prayer with their hands folded and their stone wings immobile against the bright sky.

The sun is so bright now that I have to shield my eyes in order to look over at them.

It takes a moment for them to adjust to the light and then several things happen that I don't properly register until seconds later because I'm too busy straining my eyes.

The organ music in the church stops.

The birds seem to have gone away.

The buzzing noise surges up for a moment like it's in my ears and then it too just stops.

I steady myself on a stone next to me and then I become aware that two people are standing about twenty feet in front of me.

'Oh it's them,' I say to myself.

Phew!

It's all right. I've seen these two nice old ladies before. It takes me a moment to work out where, and then I remember.

Standing by the fireplace in Weston Manor.

Well, they must be local because here they are again, chatting away to one another and standing either side of a tall gravestone.

My feet make a crunch on some twigs and one of the women stops her conversation and looks over to where I'm standing.

'Hi,' I say. 'Are you visiting the manor again? I saw you the other day in the hall. I think Dawn let you in early by mistake?'

The white-haired woman smiles in my direction in a vague sort of way, as if she's not sure who I am, and then returns to her conversation.

'Oh well,' I mutter to myself. 'Suppose I shouldn't interrupt.'

I turn away to head out of the churchyard but before I do, something kind of nags and worries at my brain and I realise what it is. The two old ladies are not only wearing exactly the same dark suits and patent heels that they were the other day, but they are standing in the same position, as if they were still stood either side of a fireplace rather than a tombstone.

My ears are ringing. I shake my head and walk out of the churchyard.

'Must stop listening to music so loud,' I say to myself.

As soon as I say 'music' I become aware that the organ tape has started up again and the birds are twittering away all around me.

I turn back towards the churchyard but the two old ladies must have already left.

As I re-enter the back grounds of the manor I see the flower lady from inside the church come out and get on her bicycle. She gives me a friendly wave as she passes by.

OK. So I've met three nice ladies. Nothing to worry about.

I turn back to the manor and realise that I've never explored the walled garden opposite the old church.

I trot down a flight of steps which end in two ornate stone urns overflowing with trailing orange and red flowers and I wander up and down the straight paths and study the old sundial in the middle of the little garden.

It's very peaceful in here.

I come across a dark little corner studded with tiny arched gravestones up against the brick wall and I stop.

This must be the pet cemetery that Dad told me about.

The inscriptions are so faded with weathering and age that I can't make out many of the names, but one of the little stones seems easier to read so I stop and say the words out loud:

'Here lies Tatters. Not that it matters.'

I smile.

So the Victorians did have a sense of humour then. Even Lady Thomas-Fulford must have had one, or else why would she allow one of her beloved dogs to be buried with this funny little rhyme on his tombstone?

I wonder if 'Tatters' is a dog in one of the

oil portraits that hangs on the dark staircase and I shudder again.

'You're better off out here, mate, I reckon,' I say to Tatters before I head back off round to the front of the house.

Odd.

The entrance door is wide open and there's no sign of life.

My heart starts to thud hard in my chest.

The door is always either firm shut or else a security guard like Sid stands by the open door, making sure that no unwanted visitors come in from the gardens and steal silver from the entrance hall.

There's no Sid to be seen.

Dawn must be covering for him, I decide. Perhaps he's gone off to help Dad.

'He– hello?' I say in a wobbly voice quite unlike my own as I climb the steps, pass the shoe-scraper and the old umbrella stand, and enter the large entrance hall of Weston Manor.

Dawn isn't there. She must have gone home early.

Her desk isn't there either. There's a huge oak dresser in its place. Somebody from the council must be experimenting with the furniture.

And somebody's lit the fire in the hall.

Weird. I've never seen it working before. Orange flames leap and crackle in the grate.

All I can hear is the ticking of the old grandfather clock at the far end of the hall.

The rest of the house is quiet. Dead quiet.

It doesn't last long.

As I stand by the door wondering what on earth I should do about closing it, something bashes against my legs and runs straight past me into the hallway.

A small black dog.

'Hello,' I say, smiling.

The dog yaps and belts through the hallway and out of sight.

And then it starts.

Bells.

One after another after another.

The noise is coming from the basements below.

I wonder whether it's some sort of fire alarm and whether I should go and get Mum. This seems like the safest thing to do so I'm heading along the downstairs corridor and past the closed door of the big dining room when there's an almighty shout from inside that room.

'You! *Here!*' shouts a male voice.

The bells intensify in volume until I'm forced to press my hands over my ears whilst with my leg I'm kicking at the door of our flat and yelling for Mum.

And then I see.

It's not the door of our flat.

It's a thin green door and this time when I push with my foot, the whole thing swings open and I can see it's not our flat inside, either.

Our kitchen isn't there any more. All I can see are more doors.

'You. *Here!*' comes the voice again. I think it's coming from the dining room but I can't be sure and I'm not going to stick my head in there.

I race back down the corridor with my arms pressed over my ears to block out the bell chorus and the sound of the man, and I run out, the heavy front door slamming behind me. I bolt into the fresh air, down the drive and away from the manor as fast as I can possibly run.

I run until I reach the bus stop and then I throw myself down on to the orange plastic seat and try to catch my breath.

I sit with my back to the manor and I wait.

I must have fallen into a bit of a trance because I jolt awake to the sound of my name being called and there's Dad in the car screeching to a halt outside the bus stop and I leap up from my seat like I've been electrocuted. I'm in the car before you can say 'weird afternoon' and Dad's giving me a big hug.

'We were worried about you!' he says. 'Your Mum said you never came home after school. She's been beside herself, she really has.'

A dark cloud passes over the sun and casts a shadow on to the front of the car. Dad indicates and turns into the manor's drive.

'What do you mean?' I say. 'I came home. The front door was wide open and there was nobody there at all. And Mum wasn't in the flat either. The flat wasn't even there!'

Dad groans and rubs his arm across his eyes when I say this.

'You're talking rubbish,' he says. 'I'm wondering if you've got sunstroke or something.'

We walk up the steps to the manor and Dad greets the security guard standing in the open doorway and ushers me inside.

'I'm just finishing up,' says Dawn from the reception desk. She piles up some guidebooks and locks them in the cupboard behind her. 'There are a couple of visitors about to come up from the basements but that's it for today.'

I stare at her without blinking.

'You...' I say, but I can't find the words.

'Are you all right, Tabitha?' she says with a worried look at Dad.

Dad shepherds me past the reception desk.

'I think she's just under exam stress,' he says.

Haha. That's a joke. I haven't even started my revision yet.

I let Dad guide me down the hall and towards our flat with its brown door and gold plate outside, and Mum tells me off, yells at me and then bursts into tears and flings her arms around me.

I eat dinner like a robot and even though Jake has texted me and asked me out and I do really, really want to see his nice normal face, it doesn't seem important compared to the whirl inside my head. So I go and lie on my bed and try to sort out the mass of thoughts that are spinning around in my brain but I can't sleep, so I get up again and go back into the kitchen.

Dad is doing some accounts at the table. He's got his black specs on and he looks so normal and Dad-like that I get the urge to cry.

I don't cry much though. Crying is for

175

babies. Ben used to cry a lot when he was little. I never did.

But I want to know why all these strange things are happening to me so I make a hot chocolate, all casual, and I wait until Dad looks up and gives me his twinkling smile, and then I say: 'Dad, does anybody ever ring the bells here? Like for a fire alarm or anything.'

Dad stretches his arms behind his head and removes his glasses. He rubs at the furrow between his eyes like it's hurting him and then he looks at me in a tired sort of way.

'Tabs, you've got to stop all this right now,' he says. 'The manor is a perfectly nice, safe place to live and the sooner we all get on with things, the better.'

'But DO they, Dad?' I persist. 'Please – it's important.'

Dad picks up his keys and his torch and passes me my slippers and a coat.

'Come on,' he says. 'If you're that interested, I'll show you.' Despite himself he's getting excited again. Dad just can't help loving his job.

He checks that Mum is sleeping first.

'She's had one of her pills,' he says. 'She won't wake up until tomorrow.'

I check in on Ben and then we head off outside into the dark corridors of Weston Manor.

I hold Dad's arm as tight as I dare.

Dad leads me down a rickety flight of steps into the basements.

'It's a bit damp down here,' he says. 'Imagine what the poor servants had to put up with. No heating or electric lighting in those days.'

I shudder.

We walk halfway down a corridor with cold stones underfoot and then Dad stops.

He points his torch upwards towards the

ceiling and my heart gives a little jolt.

There's a line of old black bells hanging side by side. Each one is attached to a cord, which seems to disappear off into the ceiling.

'They used to be attached to the bell pulls in all the rooms upstairs,' says Dad. 'But in the thirties the family installed a new electric system and they stopped using these ones.'

I stare up at the bells.

'So – so, these don't work any more?' I say.

Dad laughs and walks along to the back door. He pulls a piece of wire next to it and the largest bell clangs above me and makes me jump.

'That's the only one that's still connected,' he says. 'Tradesman's entrance. The others have had their wires to the rooms cut a long time ago.'

I try to recall what I heard this afternoon.

There's no way that all that noise could have come from one bell.

I lose my balance a bit and clutch at the wall.

'Steady on,' says Dad. His voice is concerned now. 'I'm not sure you're one hundred per cent recovered from your fall the other day. Let's go back up now.'

I want to ask him about the shouting that I heard this afternoon but one look at Dad's stern face and I know that if I risk it he'll get so concerned that I'll probably find myself whisked off to a mental hospital or something, so I keep it buttoned.

Sid, I reckon to myself as we go back upstairs to the flat. Sid said that there were things he could tell me.

I make a mental note to go and find him after school tomorrow and ask him some questions.

Then I go to bed and fall into a black

sleep almost straight away.

I wake in a sudden cold sweat in the middle of the night. The bells are ringing again, fainter than they were earlier but still loud enough that I can hear at least six separate tones all going at once.

I pull the duvet up over my head, stick in my earplugs and drift into a restless sleep.

Chapter Eleven

Mum keeps me off school the next day.
'You don't look well,' she says.

I'm too tired to protest.

Besides, I've got a plan.

I'm going to ring Gran. And I'm going to talk to Sid.

Dad goes off whistling, to get on with his job, and Mum insists that I'm tucked up on the sofa with a pillow and a soft pink blanket.

'I'm popping to the shops,' she says. 'I won't be long.'

I wait until she's gone and Ben is busy playing with Lego on the floor. Then I grab the phone.

It rings three times and then Gran's thin voice answers.

'Hi Gran,' I say. 'It's Tabs. I want to ask your advice.'

'Tabs!' says Gran. I can tell she's pleased to hear from me. We can only call her when Dad isn't around cos he thinks she's a batty old witch. 'What's it like living in the manor? Have you settled in?'

I lie back on the sofa with the phone tucked under my chin and I tell Gran everything that has happened. She won't laugh at me, Gran. She takes these things seriously.

When I've finished she draws in her breath and then lets out a wavery sigh.

'I tell you what I think, girl,' she says. 'I think . . .'

There's a crackling on the line like somebody rustling a crisp packet.

'Gran!' I yell. 'Don't go!'

But the crackling gets louder until I have to hang up. I redial straight away but there's no ring on the other end at all.

Just silence.

My heart plummets.

No Gran. And my nose has started bleeding again. I try the line again.

Nothing.

I plug my nose up and lie in front of some rubbish on TV and after a while my eyelids droop and I fall into a sleep like black velvet.

I sleep so hard that I don't even dream.

When I wake up Mum's bustling around in the kitchen again and she's made me some mushroom soup.

'There, you look brighter already,' she says. 'Good girl. Will you be all right for an hour or two if I have my nap? Dad will probably pop in and check on you later.'

'Yeah, I'll be fine,' I say. 'Don't forget your tablet.'

Mum sighs and comes back in, fills a glass with water and pops a tiny pill into her mouth. I know that she'll be asleep in ten minutes flat.

'See you later,' she says. 'Hope you won't be lonely.'

I smile.

'Well, I've got Ben, haven't I?' I say, but she's disappeared off down the hallway and I hear the soft click of her door shutting – and the sigh that means she's slipped underneath the blankets and is heading for oblivion.

I ask if Ben wants to play a board game with me but he's not interested, so I go into my room and play CDs for a while. But then I get bored, so I go over and look out of the window at the back lawn.

It's another beautiful day and the sun is streaking across the mown grass in jagged black stripes. Visitors sit on the benches at the back of the house and pour themselves cold drinks from bottles and flasks. Others wander around the kitchen gardens or the ruined stables or the graveyard behind the little church.

There's a familiar-looking person at the end of the garden, smoking a cigarette and patrolling back and forth.

Sid! He's on his lunch break. Now maybe I can get the answers to some of my zillions of questions.

I pop my head into Mum's bedroom and say, 'Mum. I'm going out for a bit. OK?' but there's no reply, just as I knew there wouldn't be.

Oh well. I did try to tell her. Not my fault if she wakes up and I'm not there.

'I won't be long,' I say to Ben. 'Stay in here and don't answer the door.'

I head out of the flat and pass the groups of visitors hanging about in the entrance hall, buying tickets or standing at the foot of the stairs admiring the oil paintings. I nod hello to Dawn and go out of the front door and round the side of the manor into the back garden.

Sid's quite a way off and I don't think he can see me, so I wave and he turns and looks in my direction. But he doesn't wave back, so I wave again and shout, 'Sid!' but still he doesn't react, which is a bit odd.

As I get closer I realise that Sid has stopped moving. He's rooted to the spot, staring at me.

'Hi!' I call. 'It's a nice day to have lunch out here, isn't it?'

He doesn't reply. Just stares at me with his mouth slightly ajar and his eyes huge.

I get a sinking feeling.

Why is he just staring at me? At least – I THINK he's staring at me.

It's gone quiet. So quiet that the birds have stopped. I can smell lavender.

'Sid?' I say, reaching him at last. 'What's the matter? Should I get Dad?'

His face contorts into an ugly grimace and his eyes almost come out of their sockets. With an effort he lifts one finger and points it just behind where I'm standing.

I have no time to turn and look at what he's pointing at because he lets out a cry and he clutches at his chest and starts to bend over, grey in the face.

Then he's falling towards me and I'm being crushed by the bulk of him and I'm aware that there are people in summer shorts and skirts running towards us at top speed and as I turn to scream at them for help I see, just for a second, a whisk of black silk dress disappearing very slowly in the opposite direction through the arch at the side of the house and there's that strange buzzing noise in my ears again but this time I manage not to faint and I stay with

Sid until Dad runs over the lawn clutching his walkie-talkie and crouches down next to us.

Mum comes out in her dressing gown almost as pale as Sid and she takes me back up to the flat and hugs me to her.

'You poor thing,' she keeps saying. 'Oh you poor thing.'

She forces me to drink a brandy and then she makes me go to bed and take one of her pills so that I'm asleep within about three minutes. I don't wake up until it's getting dark outside.

I stagger into the kitchen all disorientated and thirsty from the brandy and pill, so Mum makes me some tea and then Dad comes back in from the hospital with his head bowed and his face lined and serious.

He looks at Mum and then at me where I'm sitting in pyjamas on the sofa with Ben tucked up next to me.

'Sid had a heart attack, Tabs,' says Dad.

'He's lucky to be alive. He's got to stay in hospital for a while and then spend some time recuperating at home.'

'Is he going to come back to work after that?' I say. Visions of Sid's kind face and shiny head well up, making me want to cry.

Dad's face falls.

'I don't think so,' he says. 'He wasn't well enough to say very much, but one thing he did say to me is that he's had enough of the manor.'

'Why?' is the only word I can get out of my mouth. That one word seems to sum up everything that has happened to me at Weston Manor.

Dad thinks that I'm asking why Sid is fed up with the manor, but I think I can already guess the answer to that.

No – what I mean is:

Why did we have to come and live here?
Why are all these horrid things happening?

Why do most of them happen to me?

And why won't anyone believe me?

The only person who believed me was Sid.
And he's not coming back.

Chapter Twelve

Something tried to silence Gran – and then Sid.

Or someone.

And in the days after Sid's heart attack it's like they're out to get me too.

Not just in the daytime, but at night too.

I can't talk to my parents about it. Dad just laughs it off and Mum gets her anxious look on and tells me to 'Stop That Right Away!' or 'Don't Start That Again, Tabitha'.

Dawn changes the subject when I ask her if she's ever seen anything in the manor.

And Sid's wife calls by to see Dad and sort

out his final salary payment but I can't very well start pestering her with questions – so I don't. I just watch her trying not to cry, and Mum trying to comfort her, and I feel sad and small.

And scared.

It's started to happen in the flat too.

I thought the flat was my sanctuary. I thought I'd be safe here. I didn't think they'd get to me in here as well.

It's two days after Sid's heart attack and I'm up in my room.

I've tried calling Gran again but I can't ever seem to get through.

It's dark outside and I'm huddled under my duvet with the bedside lamp on, trying to read a diary about a teenage princess cos all my other books are about teenage vampires and that's the last thing I need to be reading at the moment. Although the diary is funny and as light as marshmallow, I can't concentrate on it and I'm drained of all energy. So I click my light off and bury myself under the pillow, trying not to listen to Mum and Dad arguing in low angry voices in the kitchen.

I expect they're arguing about me. Again.

This has been going on since even before we came to Weston Manor, but it's got a lot worse over the last few days.

I hug my pillow and close my eyes, trying to block out the noise of my fighting parents.

I must have dozed off because it feels much later when I come round to the sound of somebody whispering my name.

I jump and shoot upwards into a sitting position, clutching my duvet to my face. Like that's going to protect me. Stupid.

I click on my bedside lamp with fumbling hands and look at the clock.

It's just gone 3 a.m.

There's a rustling noise in the corner.

I freeze and glance towards the bedroom door.

Should I get up and run across the room and out to Mum and Dad?

The rustle happens again and a dark shape shifts and moves on the old armchair in the corner of my bedroom.

My eyes adjust to the light.

There's a woman sitting on my chair and she's got her head buried in her hands. I hear the faint sound of sobbing. Not close, like somebody's in my room, but like it's coming down a tunnel from miles away or from a television with the sound almost turned right down.

My ears begin to buzz and I shake my head left and right, trying to rid myself of the noise and the vision.

Maybe I'm dreaming. I pinch my arm hard but it hurts like hell. I open my mouth to shout but nothing will come out, however hard I try.

The woman stops sobbing and lifts her head from her hands. In the dim light I see the moon-shaped oval of her face.

The slits for eyes.

The face without a mouth.

She's looking right at me.

It's the same woman I saw in the dining room, the woman in the dark blue dress.

Although every fibre of my body is screaming out in terror, some small part of my brain tells me that if she's crying and looks frightened then maybe she's not out to cause me harm.

I find my voice.

'Are – are you OK?' I say. Like you do, when you've got an apparition in your bedroom!

The woman continues to stare at me and her narrow eyes bore into my skull and my ears fizz and crackle. She looks as if she is about to speak but a bell rings from somewhere in the manor and we both jump out of our skin.

'You. *Here!*' yells a sharp female voice from the dark bowels of the manor. The woman gets up and drifts out through the door.

The door is closed.

I lie for a while trying to calm my thumping heart. I can hear faint noises from far off in the big house. It sounds like two women having an argument – but as if they're having it underwater.

I lie for what feels like a lifetime, too afraid to move before at last I creep into Mum and Dad's bedroom and put my sleeping bag on the floor again.

Then I lie there wide awake until daylight.

*

Mum decides that I need to have next week off school.

'No,' I protest. 'I really, really want to go back.'

I've missed so much of the summer term already. I really want to be back to a normal place with kids yelling and fighting and teachers giving me detention.

I want to see Gemma and talk to her about normal things like music and make-up and cats and telly.

And Jake.

I really need him now. It's weird – he's stopped being annoying and is starting to represent sanity. After all, he's kind and loyal and I think I can trust him.

Mum's got her stubborn expression on so I know I'm not going to win this one.

I slump on the sofa in the lounge and text Gem.

Olds keeping me in, I put. *And they're arguing all the time. T.*

That's a bit of an understatement. Mum and Dad are hardly speaking to one another.

The Mayor is coming for a special visit today and Dad insists that I help him pick flowers from the walled garden and arrange them in large blue-and-white vases on the dining-room table where there's a huge spread of buffet food brought in by a local firm.

We finish arranging the flowers and as the house is closed to visitors for the special occasion, there's nobody much around for a few hours. Dad drives off into town to get his hair cut for the occasion and Dawn has disappeared too.

The entrance hall is deep and silent. Only the dull tick of the grandfather clock penetrates the vast space. I stand there on my own for a full five minutes, listening.

Nothing.

It's very quiet in the manor today. I wish I could say that this was a good thing, but it isn't. It's like the air is weighted with expectation and starting to build up in tension. I rub my temples where my head is starting to ache.

Just to prove that I'm not scared standing here on my own, I do a spot of whistling and then I text Gemma to ask if she ever bought the pair of leggings she'd seen in town and then I even stroll up and down the hall a bit, gazing at the paintings of Eleanor and Charles and the two beautiful half-sisters, and peering into glass cases at tiny china snuff boxes and pieces of priceless crystal.

'I live here and I am going to like it,' I say, all of a sudden. 'It's kind of my home, now. I belong here.'

I hadn't even meant to say that. It just came out.

There's a loud slam. The door to Lady Eleanor's morning room has just banged shut.

I look around the hall again. Nothing's changed. I can see a couple of photographers from the *Gazette* outside on the front lawn setting up cameras and this gives me confidence, even though a big part of me wants to run and hide away in our flat for the rest of the day to sit with Ben or Mum and try to pretend that everything is OK. But I guess there's still this mad curious and annoying part of Tabitha Grey that wants to dig deeper.

Sometimes I hate being like that. Why can't I just let things go?

'All right,' I say. It seems to help if I speak out loud to myself. It's like having a confident, bossy teacher in tow, telling me what to do next.

I look out at the men on the lawn once more for comfort and then I take a deep steadying breath and put my hand on the knob of the morning-room door.

Can't believe you're doing this, says a scared voice inside me.

'Neither can I,' I mutter, but by then I've pushed the door open.

There's an abrupt rustle as I enter the room, like somebody's just stood up in a hurry. Out of the corner of my eye I see something dark swish out of sight. Then a heavy silence falls on the room. I walk to the centre and look out of the sash window over the gardens of the manor.

'Good,' I say. I can see Dad making his way up the drive. He's got a special jaunty walk that I can spot a mile off, both hands tucked into his jeans and his head nodding a bit from side to side.

It gives me more strength to see Dad. I turn away from the window and face the middle of the room again. I look around at all the pictures crammed in here. There are tiny black-and-white photographs of people in oval frames over the fireplace. On the walls there are larger photographs of houses in Madeira and London. Dad told me that the Thomas-Fulfords had several homes in addition to Weston. And dotted around the wallpapered walls are pencil drawings and oil paintings of various members of the family.

There's even one of Lady Eleanor as a little girl.

'She was pretty then,' I say, before I can help myself. I swear I hear a snort. Kind of like a horse, but fainter. I move away from the wall and back into the room.

Something moves with me.

It's not something I can see.

It's a smell.

It's like lavender but mixed with perfume so strong and acidic that I nearly keel over. I sniff my own wrist to check that it's not me, although I know full well that the body spray I got from Superdrug smells nothing like that, and then I hunt all round the room looking for air fresheners and bowls of potpourri and sniffing the furniture to see if it smells of some weird polish or something. But the smell just gets stronger and stronger where I am until it's like I'm standing in the middle of some moving tornado of scent.

'Get a grip,' I say to myself. 'It's just a smell. Smells can't hurt you.'

I glance out of the window to see where Dad has got to and my heart leaps with relief when I see him pounding up the lawn towards the arch at the side of the house.

While I'm looking at Dad, the smell moves.

I follow it.

It moves over to Lady Eleanor's writing desk and hovers in the air over her chair. The air in the room hangs heavy and hot. It's like the room is getting smaller and darker and stuffier and the ceiling is moving down to try and squash all the air out of the room. My head is pounding now, like a migraine or something, and my heart keeps doing funny flutters in my chest.

Then it goes.

Just like that. The smell lifts and disappears and the room seems to get brighter and lighter again.

I walk towards the door with my heart pounding and I try as usual not to look sideways in the tiny mirror on the panelling just inside the door as I go past it, but I swear I see both my own profile go past and then another taller one close up behind me.

My neck prickles with ice.

'Dad!' I yell as he comes through into the entrance hall, opening the big front door and allowing sunlight to flood over the parquet floor. 'You're back!'

Dad grins.

'Well, I live here,' he says. 'Of course I'm back! Are you ready for today, Tabs?'

I'm not sure what I'm ready for at the moment but I smile and link my arm through his. My heart starts to calm down a bit.

'Bring it on!' I say.

The house changes with all the people rushing about.

I'm in the grounds outside and I'm looking up at the front of the house, like I did on the very first day we came here.

More press have turned up so there are loads of bored-looking men with cameras hanging about smoking on the steps to the manor.

I stare up at the shuttered windows on the first floor. Since Sid left, things only get done at the last moment and usually by some sort of relief security guard drafted over from another of the council's buildings.

The house looks down on me. Sometimes I swear it's about to speak.

The walls gleam white in the sun and the glass windows that line the verandah sparkle through their stained glass colour panes.

Groups of birds chatter and swoop in the bushes at the sides of the house and there's the sharp click of croquet balls at the back and the roar and rush of traffic piling up outside on Weston Drove.

It all seems so normal.

The house looks stripped of character today, like a square white cake plonked down on a green iced base.

It's like – the more people pour in and out of the doors, the less the house has its personality any longer.

I think what it's like in the evenings when all the visitors have gone and I shudder and get up from the old flight of steps on the circular front lawn.

Time to help Dad again.

It's kind of good that there are all these people knocking about. I reckon nothing will happen whilst there are so many loud modern bodies all over the place, filling up the grand rooms and the huge entrance hall with noise and gaiety.

Dad gives a speech to welcome the mayor and then people descend on the buffet lunch in the dining room in front of the cases of Chinese lions. The room looks so beautiful that for one short moment I feel pleased to be living in the manor – but that doesn't last long.

'Tabs, I'd like you to show the mayor and his guests around the house, please,' says Dad.

I stop with a sausage roll halfway to my mouth.

What?

'No, I can't,' I stumble. 'I don't want to go upstairs.'

Dad smiles at the mayor with this big fake 'What can I do about my daughter?' look and then pulls me off by the arm into a corner of the hall.

'You've got to stop this nonsense,' he says. 'The mayor is our distinguished guest. You're to take him round the house, and that's that.'

I can see that any more argument would be pointless, so I drag my feet back into the dining room and put on my polite smile.

The mayor and his four guests follow me

into the drawing room, where I point out the valuable Wedgwood collection and the unusual porcelain lamps, and then into the entrance hall where they gaze up at the portraits of Sir Charles and Lady Thomas-Fulford and admire the beauty of the half-sisters, Lucinda and Rose.

I reach the foot of the staircase and for once I don't go all cold, so I take a deep breath and take slow, creaking steps up to the first-floor landing, talking all the way about the things Dad has taught me.

I show them Lady Eleanor's bedroom and the guest bedroom next door. I even manage the library, without passing out or smelling anything weird.

Then I reach Sir Charles Thomas-Fulford's bedroom and I'm looking forward to showing the visitors those weird bell pulls by the bed and the special lever for shutting the bedroom door without getting out of bed . . . but I can't.

The door's closed.

I push it and twiddle with the doorknob but I can't shift it.

'Never mind,' says the mayor, polite as ever. 'We can still enjoy the other rooms.'

I turn away from the door but as I move back towards the mayor there's a loud groan.

It's coming from inside Sir Charles' bedroom.

I look wide-eyed at the visitors but they're chatting amongst themselves.

There's a clunk somewhere near the door.

The door swings open about an inch and then stops.

'You need to get someone to look at that!' says the mayor. His party all laugh.

I take them inside with my breath held. But everything in there looks the same as normal, so I explain about the shaving mirror and let them enjoy the views out towards the back lawns.

We go through to the two servants' bedrooms that are on the same floor as the grand bedrooms and, like all visitors, the mayor comments on the fact that it was pretty unusual for servants to have bedrooms so close to their mistress and master and I nod and smile, and all the time I try not to look out at the croquet lawn outside or think about bells or smells. It must be working because actually our tour of the rooms upstairs and even the poky rooms in the top-floor attic goes without a hitch, and by the time we get back to the first-floor landing and I stop them by the grandfather clock to tell them a bit about it, I'm starting to think that perhaps Dad is right and I've been a bit over-imaginative lately. I'm thinking that I ought to try and do something nice for him later when a woman rushes up to our group and heads straight into the servants' toilet on this floor. She doesn't catch my eye but I get a whiff of her strange odour and I reckon she's one of the catering staff cos she smells of kitchen cleaner and meat and isn't dressed like the other visitors, so although that toilet is not usually open to the public I guess that this is a special occasion. I ignore her and then I continue talking to the mayor and his guests just outside, answering their questions about the house.

When I've finished ten minutes later the toilet door is still firmly shut but one of the mayor's party is shifting from leg to leg and looking pointedly at the door.

'Is there still somebody in there? Do you think they've collapsed?' says a lady in a violet suit with black-rimmed glasses. 'Perhaps we should knock?'

I nod and tap very softly on the door, and

then a bit louder when there's no reply.

'Why don't you go downstairs and use the visitor lavatories there?' I say, because the guest is looking as if he's about to burst.

I watch the party go down the dark staircase, chatting amongst themselves and I feel proud of myself for a moment.

I gave a talk about the house and people enjoyed it.

And nothing happened, more to the point.

Except I've maybe got an unconscious member of staff on my hands now.

Dad's given me one of his walkie-talkies so I press the button like he's shown me and after a moment or two he comes bounding up the stairs in his usual way, two at a time.

'Dad, you've got lipstick on your cheek,' I say.

Dad laughs and wipes it off.

'Never mind that,' he says. 'What's going on up here?'

I point at the door of the servants' toilet.

'You shouldn't really let people use this,' sighs Dad. 'It's part of the visitor exhibit.'

I roll my eyes.

'Dad, there is a LADY stuck in there,' I say. 'She might be ill. Or dead. Could you please stop telling me off and DO something?'

Dad knocks twice on the door but there's no reply. 'Stand back,' he says, just like men do in films. Then he runs at the door and kicks it open with his boot. The door flies open with a bang, hitting the wall inside.

There's nobody there.

I go in and look up at the window.

It's tiny, only big enough for a cat to squeeze through and not a solid-looking woman.

Even Dad looks a bit confused.

'Are you SURE that she went in there, Tabs?' he says.

'Yes,' I say. 'She was in a hurry.'

'Well,' says Dad. 'She must have somehow got out again without you seeing.'

'Not possible,' I say. 'I was standing right here all the time. And how do you explain the door being locked from the inside?'

I can see Dad struggling to explain this one, but his radio crackles into life again and it's Dawn telling him to come back downstairs. So he bounds off again and I follow because I don't want to be left up here with all the empty four-poster beds and the library.

For the rest of the afternoon I hand round plates of sandwiches and top up glasses of wine and champagne and I watch Mum making a big effort to talk to guests. I admire her pale-pink lip gloss and her shiny brown bun and the way that she's managed to dress in a floaty lilac top and leggings and still look a million times more classy than Dawn with her flashy lipstick and tight top.

Dawn is over in the corner of the dining room by the Chinese lions surrounded by the press from the local paper.

Dad keeps looking over at her with a sour expression on his face.

I'm pretty sure Mum sees.

After a while she excuses herself and goes back to the flat where Ben has been left locked in on his own with me checking him every half hour and to the safety of her sleeping pills and bedroom.

By six o'clock the guests have all gone and the caterers have come in to clean up the mess. Dad supervises them and I go back to the flat to tell Ben all about the afternoon.

He listens with his eyes wide, as usual. He's too little to be trusted at these posh events. There's always the risk that he'll charge into somebody's legs and cause them to drop their food or hide behind a chair and leap out, giving some old man a heart attack.

'There's a lot of stuff going on here, Ben,' I say after I've told him about the guests. 'A lot of stuff that I don't understand.'

He tucks his little hand into mine and we watch some rubbish reality TV programme about people learning to be opera stars until Dad comes back in much later to cook us omelettes for supper. Mum surfaces and gives us a tight smile and skirts around Dad without touching him or talking to him and surely she must be able to smell what I smell?

Perfume.

Dad smells of Dawn's perfume.

That night my father sleeps on the couch.

Chapter Thirteen

Jake comes to visit.

Mum says it's OK so I spend all Friday morning getting ready in my bedroom.

I really want to make more effort with Jake now. I feel like I've been taking him for granted and Gemma agrees. So I've texted him loads this week and he's replied to most of them.

I look at my pale reflection and lank hair in the mirror and something in me kind of snaps.

I'm fed up being tired and stressed and anxious.

I reach for a red dress that Mum bought me but that I haven't yet worn. It's short and flippy and has two spaghetti straps. I put on black ballerinas and then I reach for my make-up case and add a bright red lipstick and dark eyeliner.

I dry my hair upside down until it stands out in a dark blonde cloud around my head and then I survey the results in the mirror.

A different sort of girl stares back at me.

Tabitha, definitely. Not Tabs. Not today. I look about five years older than usual.

I top the look off with some mascara and spray shine stuff all over my head and then I float into the lounge for Mum's approval.

'Oh!' she says, looking a bit shocked. Then she sees my expression and smiles.

'You look nice, Tabitha,' she says. 'I like it when you make a bit of an effort with your appearance. Very striking.'

I glow. It's not often that Mum praises me these days.

Ben giggles so I know I must look kind of OK.

Dad pops back at coffee time.

'Since when did you start wearing after-shave?' Mum asks him. 'No, it's all right. Don't answer that.'

She goes off down to the basement, clutching her pointe shoes in their pink box.

Dad looks kind of flustered and his cheeks are redder than usual. He doesn't even go on about my outfit being too old for me, which is unusual.

'I won't be coming back for lunch today,' is all he says. 'All right?'

I nod.

This means I get Jake all to myself. He won't mind Ben, but the main thing is that my warring parents will not be around. Mum will be asleep and Dad will be – doing whatever Dad is doing. I don't want to think too much about that.

I'm ready way too early. Jake isn't due for another hour so I pace up and down in the flat, checking my reflection every two minutes and re-applying lip gloss. At last I see him coming up the semi-circular drive and gazing up at the house like people always do when they visit for the first time. A few minutes later there's a soft knock on the flat door and he's standing there, all clean-smelling and tall with his fierce blue eyes smiling down at me.

'Hi,' he says. 'I bought you these.'

He holds out a pile of DVDs and a bag of Maltesers.

I blush.

'Come in,' I say. 'D'you want a coffee?'

Jake's staring at me like I'm a stranger.

'You look different,' he says. 'You don't usually wear that sort of lipstick, do you?'

I grin.

'Like it?' I say. I'm determined to be flirty and confident today. I'm not letting the house get to me and I'm going to make Jake see that I'm exciting and fun to be with.

'Erm, yes,' says Jake in a polite voice. 'I think so. Nice dress.'

I flick my hair back and put instant into two cups, all the while watching him look around our flat.

'This is really cool,' he says. 'I didn't think it would be so big.'

'Well, it's not really, compared to the rest of the house,' I say. 'Maybe I'll take you round later if you'd like?'

I don't really want to. But everybody who comes here wants The Tour, and I'd rather do it myself than have to cringe watching Dad do it, all puffed up and self-important.

I figure that if Jake is with me, I'll be safe.

*

I make us a pile of cheese sandwiches and fetch juice from the fridge and we sit down with Ben and watch a DVD about a man and a woman who are destined never to meet. It's quite funny and even Ben laughs a bit. For a moment I forget where I am and just enjoy sitting next to Jake with his arm pressed up against mine and when he thinks I'm not looking I watch him sideways out of the corner of my eye and enjoy the way that his eyes crinkle at the corners when he laughs.

We're so engrossed in the film that we jump when Mum comes in from downstairs, her cheeks flushed and her eyes lit up in that peculiar way that only comes from her dancing.

'Hi Jake,' she says. 'Good to see you. I don't know why Tabitha hardly ever has you over.'

I shoot her a furious look. Mothers are SO embarrassing.

'Sorry, Tabs,' says Mum. 'But welcome, anyway, Jake. You guys got enough food?'

I gesture at the pile of sandwiches and raise my eyebrows a few times at Mum, so she gets the hint and goes off to get changed.

'Sorry about that,' I say. 'Why are parents always so annoying?'

Then I realise what I've said and flush scarlet. Jake only has a dad. His mum died when he was a baby and his gran helped bring him up.

'Sorry,' I say, yet again. 'Shall I just shut up now?'

I shove a triangular sandwich in my mouth and make a face.

Jake laughs and we watch the end of the film with his arm draped around the tops of my shoulders so that I go all tingly.

Mum comes back into the room dressed in jeans and a khaki jacket and with her rucksack on her back.

'Going food shopping,' she announces. 'Be good. And – Tabitha?'

I twist my neck to look round at her.

'Yeah?'

'You know I love you heaps, don't you?' she says.

Omigod.

Why do parents always have to say these things at the worst possible moments?

'Yeah, yeah,' I mumble, turning my face away from Jake so that he can't see my unattractive red burning face.

Mum gives me another look, which I can't work out at all, and then she slips out of the flat with Ben hanging off her skirts.

'She's nice, your mum,' Jake says. 'Pretty. And kind, I reckon. I wish I still had my mum sometimes.'

This is so unexpected coming from a BOY

that I nearly choke on my cheese and pickle.

I stare at Jake's chiselled features and I think: *Perhaps I could love you after all.*

When I've washed up the plates and Jake's dried them, I take a deep breath and ask if he'd like the tour of the manor now.

He nods, so we lock up the flat and head off down the long corridor outside, with sunshine streaming through the Edwardian glass windows and lighting up bits and pieces of furniture inside the big rooms.

'Wow,' says Jake as I take him into the dining room. 'Can you imagine actually eating your dinner in here?'

I shudder. The table is laid for about twenty people with silver knives and fish knives and the glass goblets are out today too because a school group has been round on an educational trip. The Chinese lions preside over it all as usual, teeth bared into ugly snarls.

I take Jake into the elegant drawing room and he sucks his breath in sharply with admiration at the ornate furnishings and floor-to-ceiling windows that open on to the gardens of the manor.

'Wow,' he says, yet again. 'This is like SO cool. You're lucky, living here.'

As I take Jake into the trophy room and then Lady Thomas-Fulford's morning room I ponder on that statement.

I don't feel lucky at all. Just about everything's been going wrong since we moved in.

Jake admires the photos and miniature paintings in the morning room and then he stands by the desk in the corner for a moment and says: 'Can you smell lavender?'

I jump. In fact I can, but I've been trying not to notice it.

'It's the polish that the cleaners use,' I say

quickly. I do not want Jake to think of me as some ghost nut.

'And something else,' says Jake as we leave the morning room and I try not to glance in the little servants' mirror just by the door. 'Coal, maybe?'

Yeah. He's right. I can smell coal, just like somebody's lit an old fire somewhere nearby.

'Can't smell anything,' I mutter. 'Let's go upstairs.'

We go upstairs without pausing to look at any of the pictures of brown dogs on the panelled walls. Then I conduct a whistle-stop tour of the grand bedrooms and the servants' quarters and I don't tell Jake that in the library I get a whiff of something so vile that I nearly keel over and that in the guest bedroom something or somebody grabs hold of the back of my jeans belt and gives it a good hard tug so that I let out a shriek and have to grab on to the bed to stop falling over.

Jake appears to have forgotten about the lavender and coal smells and he doesn't pick up on anything else.

We go into Lady Thomas-Fulford's bedroom and as we pass the huge chest of drawers by the door a photograph of one of her dogs slams down hard on the wooden surface so that I jump and clutch Jake's arm.

'It's your heavy footsteps,' I say, trying to make a joke of it. 'You knocked it over.'

I let go of his arm with some reluctance. It feels nice – all muscular and real and warm beneath the sleeve of his long black top.

'Or else someone doesn't want us to be in here,' says Jake with a big grin.

I smile back. Good. He's not taking any of it seriously.

'What's this?' he asks. There's a faded album on the dressing table and Jake's turning the pages. I shoot a nervous look at the security camera.

'I don't think you should be touching that,' I say. But I'm dead nosy and I've never noticed the photo album before so I go and stand close to his shoulder, so close that I can feel the heat coming off him – and it's kind of nice.

'Loads of old dead people! Boring,' says Jake, losing interest and wandering over to look at the paintings on the other side of the room.

I flick through the pages. The photographs inside are tiny, blurred and almost all of servants posing outside in the garden at Weston Manor.

I flick through fast because Jake's getting fed up of waiting – until one of the photographs catches my eye.

A line of female servants in long dark dresses with white aprons and white frilled caps, standing in front of the old sundial which is still outside in the walled garden.

I peer closer.

There's something about the girl on the far left of the picture.

She's not smiling, for a start. The others are, but this girl has big scared eyes and her hands are clasped in front of her stomach.

It's the eyes.

I've seen them somewhere before.

Although I don't much want to, I keep turning the pages of the album and something else catches my eye.

There's a tiny faded photo of two old ladies standing by a fireplace in the hall at Weston.

I squint to read the caption.

'Lucinda and Rose,' it says. 'Return to Weston, Christmas 1945.'

There's that buzz in my ears again. It's faint this time, but it's there.

I feel dizzy, like I might pass out.

'Jake,' I say. I grab his arm and propel him out of the room. 'I'll show you the kitchens if you really want but then I think I'd like to go back to the flat.'

I drag him back on to the landing and downstairs and then I ask the new security guard, Paul, to take us down to the basement kitchens where I do my best not to look at the row of black bells hanging down in the corridor or to think about the unhappy servant girl and the two old ladies in the photograph album. I make sure that at all times I'm standing near Paul.

Jake loves it all. Loves it.

'Can I come and live here?' he says. I look at his face and it seems as if he's only half joking. 'I really, really like this place. Can't see what my gran makes all the fuss about.'

Oh yeah. Jake did tell me that his gran doesn't like the house.

That all seems months ago. But it was only a couple of weeks.

Time does funny things at Weston Manor.

Jake goes at about five after conversation between us kind of dries up. I try to talk to him about the photograph album and the woman in my bedroom and my feelings about living in this house. But he starts yawning and fidgeting and looking at me in a funny way so I shut up and after he's gone I wander around the entrance hall for a while, looking up at pictures and wondering if Mum's back yet. I catch a glance of myself in the servants' mirror outside Lady Eleanor's morning room and I decide that I do look a bit deranged with the red lipstick on so I wipe it off there and then and head outside. I don't really want to go back to the flat and sit on my own and there's something else I want to see without Jake looking at me in that odd way.

I head through the arch at the side of the manor and open the gate into the churchyard. There's nobody there today so I head right towards the spot where I saw the two old ladies talking.

They were leaning on either side of a tall gravestone topped with a large cross. I crouch down and read the inscription.

The inscription on the tomb is clear.

In loving memory of Lady Eleanor Thomas-Fulford
Died 26th June, 1933

I shiver, a great violent judder that rocks my body. Then I notice the two smaller tomb-stones just to the right of Eleanor's. One of them has been carved with elaborate flowers and buds round the inscription.

To the memory of Lucinda MacDonald of Weston
Manor
Died 17th May, 1953

Next to this stone is another of the same height but this one has a small stone angel on the top. I crouch down, even though I know what I'm going to see.

Yes.

Gone but not forgotten
In loving memory of Rose MacDonald
Died 3rd December, 1956

I get up. My legs have gone soft, like all the blood has been drained out of them.

So why – why did I see these two women the other day? Do they come every day?

There's a soft melodious laugh behind me, like somebody heard me thinking out loud and thinks that I'm stupid or something but that they're quite fond of me nonetheless.

I spin round but I know that there will be nobody there.

But something else catches my eye. On the opposite side of the path is a tiny gravestone in the shape of a cradle.

I bend over to read the inscription. There's ivy all over it so I have to poke and pull at the strands until I can make out the carved lettering.

In loving memory of Bertie Thomas-Fulford
Taken from this life aged five on 4th November,
1899

This is all getting too weird.

Who is this child? I can't recall anybody at the manor ever mentioning a child.

Still – the two old ladies looked kind enough

when I saw them before. They don't look like they're out to get me. 'Even if they're dead,' I mutter to myself. I can't quite take in what I'm saying. But it's true – they didn't look at all as if they would cause me any trouble.

Unlike their half-sister, Lady Eleanor.

I try to block the image of her stern features looking down from the painting in the hall and I head back towards the manor.

My head is whirling with stuff I don't much want to think about.

Again.

I sit in the walled garden on the way back and gaze at the pet graves again.

I find them comforting, in a way. Little dogs can't harm you, whether they're alive or dead.

Over the wall beyond the ruined greenhouses the top half of Weston rises up towards the sky.

It's almost as quiet in here as it was in the cemetery.

I look at my watch. I've got a few minutes before Mum will be looking for me.

I close my eyes in the sun and lean my head back against the wall. It's hypnotic out here, with the chirp of the birds and the hum of a lawnmower and the thud of croquet balls from the back lawn and the sun is acting like a drug on my tired sleepless brain and I start to dip into the dark as the breeze tickles my face and the sun warms my cheeks and then it all fades to a fuzz and I sink somewhere warm and soft.

A child whispers my name.

'Ben?' I say, waking up with a start and a dry throat.

There's nobody there. I must have dreamed the whisper. My head aches and I feel even more tired and like I could just lie down and sleep on the paving slabs but I drag my weary bones towards the entrance of the manor instead. Maybe I'll actually get a good night's sleep tonight.

There's a different lady on reception today. She's older than Dawn, with short grey hair and gold studs in her ears but she's wearing trendy leggings and a pinafore dress which looks a bit odd on an old person. She must be at least thirty.

'Hello, love,' she says as I flick through postcards and books. 'Can I help you? Dawn's off sick today so I've come over to cover for her. I'm Maggie.'

'I'm Tabs and I live here,' I say with a huge yawn. 'My dad's the Keeper.'

The woman smiles.

'I know,' she says. 'And a very good one too, or so I've heard.'

I smile back. It's nice to hear Dad being praised for the right reasons rather than for him being tall and handsome and a hit with the ladies.

Just as we're talking about Dad he comes bounding into the entrance hall with his face flushed and his hair a bit messed up.

'The cavalry's here,' he says to the lady. 'You go home. I'll lock up.'

She reaches for her coat and heads off.

I help Dad tidy up her desk and empty the cash till and there's a bit of a silence between us and then I really want to know where he's been, so I say: 'Did you have a good day, Dad?' and he makes a big thing out of counting five pound notes for a moment. Then he turns and gives me his dazzling smile and says, 'Manor business – you know. Networking and stuff,' which doesn't really mean anything and I wish that I hadn't heard that Dawn was off today because now my mind is working overtime on things it doesn't like. But I know better than to push Dad any more because his temper can come out like a sudden sharp whoosh so I button it and follow him back to the flat.

Ben is back. He's quietly sitting in front of the television fiddling with a box of coloured bricks.

'When did Mum go out?' says Dad, filling up the kettle.

I look at the clock.

She's been out for hours.

'She must have come back while I was out and then popped out again,' I say. 'Maybe she met a friend?'

Dad looks worried now. We both know that Mum left all her friends behind in London.

'I'll get supper together and then I might go out and look for her,' he says. 'Beans on toast all right?'

I nod and pull Ben on to my lap.

'Don't worry,' I whisper to him. 'She'll be back soon. She always comes back, right?'

Me, Dad and Ben sit at the kitchen table as the light fades outside and Dad gulps his baked beans down very fast so that he can go out and look for Mum. He goes into their bedroom to get a jumper as the night's cooling down outside and then I hear a great shout and he comes out into the kitchen with a grey face and waving a piece of paper in the air.

He's rambling rubbish so I make him sit down.

Then I take the note and begin to read.

Chapter Fourteen

This is what it says:

Dear Mark,

I've decided to go and live with Mum for a while.
Please don't try to get in touch. I just need some time
away from this family and from this place. I know
you're chasing after somebody else and I can't bear to
see it happen right under my nose. So I'm going to
live with Mum for a bit and get my thoughts together.
I trust you to carry on being a good father while I'm
away.

Rachel

My legs threaten to collapse so I pull out a wooden chair and let it catch me. When I've read the letter again I look up at Dad. His face is grey and his hands are buried in his hair so that the bits between his fingers stick up in little stiff peaks.

'Is it true, Dad?' I whisper. I'm hanging on to Ben for dear life, trying to stop him crying. 'Are you chasing after somebody else? Is that why Mum's gone to live with Gran?'

Dad doesn't answer for a moment. When he lifts his head his eyes are heavy with tears, but he looks me straight in the eye and then does just what I don't really expect him to do.

He nods.

Just one short nod but it tells me everything I need to know. I grab Ben by the hand and pull him into my bedroom. Then I fling myself face-down on to the soft pillow and let all my tears and frustrations have free reign.

I cry for so long that all I can hear is my own snorts and snuffles in my ears, but when I stop at last Ben's fallen asleep and I can hear something else.

'No, no, not again,' I whisper.

The bells. They're ringing again. In a really haphazard manner.

They don't stop ringing.

All night.

There are smells around my bed.

Lavender.

Coal.

Voices whisper from the corners of my bedroom and I can hear the swish of silk going back and forth across the wooden floorboards. My windows rattle and bang and at one point something soft brushes my face and there's a loud laugh right up against my ear.

'LEAVE ME ALONE!' I yell, flapping

my arms across my face. 'WHY ARE YOU DOING THIS?'

Dad comes running in when I shout but I turn my face to the wall and tell him to go away.

I don't get a wink of sleep.

The next morning is black.

Very black.

I get out of bed and my windows are wide open and the rug on the floor is crumpled up like somebody's been rolling on it.

I look in the mirror and for a moment I don't even look like me any more but like a worn-out serving maid with straggly hair and dark rings under her eyes.

The kitchen is very quiet without Mum bustling about and making breakfast.

I pour cereal into a bowl and get some for Ben and then I leave him swinging his legs and eating. I shut myself in the bedroom and ring Gran.

'Gran, it's me,' I whisper. 'I know Mum's there. But I need to talk to you in private. Can she hear?'

There's a slight crackle on the line but Gran's still there.

'She's in the shower,' Gran says. 'What's up Tabs? I can't seem to get a good line to talk to you these days.'

I pull a face even though she can't see it.

'It's this house,' I say. 'It's making weird things happen. It's probably even made Dad and Mum fall out.'

Gran gives a snort.

'I know exactly why your parents have fallen out,' she says. 'Nothing to do with the house. It's to do with your father, Tabs.'

My stomach does an uncomfortable lurch.

Gran is always ranting on about men. And

she's never liked Dad. She says that her psychic powers told her right away that he'd cause problems.

And it seems that she's kind of right.

'Gran,' I whisper. 'I need to talk to you about what's happening here. You're the only person who won't laugh at me. You will believe me, won't you?'

I can almost see Gran smiling and brushing down the sleeves of her blue woollen cardigan.

'Always, love,' says Gran. 'You're my grand-daughter.'

So I take a deep breath and I tell her what's been happening to me and I've just got to the bit about the gravestones and I mention Lady Eleanor and the child's grave and then there's another much louder noise on the line like somebody blowing up a packet of crisps right in my ear and then there's a high-pitched scream that causes me to drop the phone and clutch my ear in pain.

When I pick it up again Gran's gone.

I redial straight away but the number just makes the engaged signal over and over, so I give up and go to check on Ben.

We sit in complete silence messing around with cornflakes and milk but not really having the heart to eat it, and then Dad comes in stretching his arms above his head.

'Right,' he says. 'It's a new day so let's try and have a new start.'

I glare at him.

How can we have a new start when Mum's not here? I hate Dad at that moment. I really hate him. I hate the way that's he woken up from a night of deep sleep and is now humming under his breath to the radio while he makes toast for himself and plans his day in the manor.

I hate that he's made a mess of everything.

And I hate that Mum is living away from us all and probably crying into Gran's arms and wondering if she'll ever come home again.

'You can do some work for me today, Tabitha,' Dad says. 'No argument, please. And Monday you'll get back to school and catch up on all the work you've missed. OK?'

I wonder what on earth we're supposed to do with Ben while we're running about the manor but as usual I'm left to sort out all the details. So I get him dressed and tell him that he's got to be good today and come with me when I go around the big house and he smiles, so I reckon it will be OK.

My mobile rings while Dad's in the shower.

'Tabs?' whispers Mum's voice. 'Hello, love. Are you OK?'

Tears well up in my eyes. My throat tightens and threatens to choke me so I nod, which is stupid because she can't see that on the phone.

'We're OK,' I say after a moment. 'I'm taking Ben to help out in the manor today.'

There's a long silence on the end of the phone. I can almost hear Mum wrestling with what to say next.

'Tabitha,' she says. 'Look after yourself. Eat properly and get an early night once in a while, will you? I'll call you every day, I promise.'

'OK,' I say in a small sad voice. 'When are you coming back?'

Another silence.

'When the time is right,' says Mum. 'When things are better. Dad will take good care of you. And Gran's taking good care of me.'

I open my mouth to ask if I can speak to Gran. Gran can make sense of everything that's happening. Gran knows stuff. I'm sure she does.

But Mum's already gone.

I sit on the edge of my bed for a moment.

The smell of lavender is very strong in here this morning. It makes me feel sick.

'Go away,' I whisper in what's left of my voice. 'Just leave me alone. Please.'

I check my phone.

Jake hasn't replied to my last text.

Dad gives me a duster this morning and instructs me to dust all the fireplace fenders.

There are a lot of fireplaces in Weston Manor so my heart sinks, but he's not in the mood to be argued with and all morning he's been jumpy, looking at his watch and then into reception where Dawn is sitting selling tickets to the visitors.

He's already come to tell me twice that he'll instruct me exactly when to come home for lunch and that I'm not to go back to the flat until then.

I'm upstairs polishing a brass fender in the

library and Ben is playing on the floor next to me when there's a loud whisper in my right ear.

'GET OUT!'

It's a man's voice.

I leap up and flee the room, coming back to grab Ben.

It's lunchtime and, despite everything, my stomach's growling.

How cross is Dad going to be if I go to start the lunch off without him?

As I pass reception I notice that the hall is deserted. There's a chill in the air – Dad's always moaning that the council cut down on heating and that visitors shouldn't be left to freeze in the house. There's someone new at the desk, an older woman, also with grey hair but tucked up in a knot at the back of her head.

I sigh. They really ought just to have one person on reception full-time. It's very confusing.

I say 'hello' to her as I go past the desk but she continues staring ahead and ignores me so I decide I'm not going to waste time speaking to a rude receptionist and I head back down the corridor to our flat.

You know when sometimes you have a bad feeling and then you ignore it? It's just a fleeting pang of something not right but you reckon you're kidding yourself so you shake your head and carry on like nothing's wrong?

That's what happens to me.

I get this real feeling of something bad about to happen and I'm wondering whether it will be the bells again or the smells or the sad lady in the blue dress and as I put my key in the door I'm thinking about all this and really hoping that it all leaves me alone and then I'm seeing two people leap apart and there's Dad and Dawn on the sofa at opposite ends pretending to be all casual and normal.

I'm still holding Ben's hand so I back away and pull him back down the corridor and out into the entrance hall of the manor and then I pull him down the steps and outside into the warm air and I can't really drag a scared little boy down a main road so I go round the side of the house and into the back gardens and find a corner of the walled garden near the dog graves where there's a bench and a lily pond and I sit there and shake and shake even though it's a hot day and Ben says nothing but just gazes up at me with big frightened eyes.

I wipe my eyes and take some deep shuddering breaths and then I stare up at the dark-green shuttered eyes of the manor and I wonder how everything can have gone so wrong.

It's very hot.

There are even crickets chirping, like in films. The air is fizzing with them.

I can hear the click and thud of croquet balls out on the main lawns and I wonder if it's the Alice in Wonderland event but I feel too dazed and shattered to move from the bench. So I carry on sitting there with Ben and wondering if Dawn has left the flat and how I'm ever going to look her in the eye again. I'm so deep in thought and half-asleep from the heat that I don't notice the man wandering past in front of me at first but it's only when he's passed through an arch into the old kitchen gardens that I realise he was wearing a flat cap and breeches and pushing a wheelbarrow full of manure. With a jolt I realise that the kitchen garden is locked and it's not the day when the manor gardeners come in and then on the hot air comes a stench of something steamy and earthy and I hear the faint whinny of a horse and I'm thinking that we don't have horses here and it's coming from the direction of the ruined stables and my skin starts to prickle and my ears buzz and I feel Ben grip my hand a little tighter so I look down at him and say, 'It's all right, Ben,' as I do about a hundred times a day and then there's a sort of misty haze right in front of me at the top of the steps into the walled garden and it turns into the figure of a woman in a black dress.

It's the woman I saw on reception.

It's the woman from my photo.

She walks down the steps, very straight and upright.

Lavender surges into my nostrils.

The sour taste of blood drips down my throat.

She walks right through the sundial in the middle of the garden.

The buzzing in my ears steps up a gear, like somebody turned up the volume dial.

The woman walks towards me.

Her feet make no sound on the paving stones.

Dark eyes glower. She stretches out her arms.

She's so close I can smell the musty lace on her black silk dress.

Ben begins to scream, great silent screams with his mouth wide open but no sound coming out. I scoop him up and just as I feel the woman bear down on top of me I duck underneath her arms and run.

I sprint from the garden and straight down the side of the manor with Ben wriggling in my arms and I don't look back, I just keep on running down the main road and I know all of a sudden where I have to go cos I sent a card there. Mum gave me the address and although it's a ten-minute bus ride I can't hang around near the manor, I've got to get away as fast as possible so I just keep running and running until I'm up the garden path of that neat modern house in the quiet close and I'm ringing the bell with a finger that's trembling so hard I can see about sixteen of them. A woman opens the door and there's a man's Geordie voice just behind her. I fall into the house and concerned arms shelter me and lead me, at last, into safety.

'Take your time, lass,' says the familiar voice. 'I'm not going anywhere.'

Chapter Fifteen

Sid's wife makes me a sugary tea and fetches me some cotton wool to plug up my nose.

'That's it,' she says in her gentle, firm voice. 'Tilt your head forwards, Tabitha.'

Ben sits on my lap. I catch a glimpse of our reflections in the mirror. We both look dead pale, like it's the middle of winter rather than a hot June afternoon.

'I – I didn't know where else to go,' I stutter through wads of cotton wool.

She nods.

'It's quite all right,' she says. 'Sid and I've been expecting you, in a way. I ought to ring your father before we talk. He'll be worried about you.'

'I doubt it,' I mutter, but she rings Dad and explains that I'm here and safe and that she will ring him again later.

She waits until I've drained my tea and goes into the kitchen to make some more.

Sid was stretched out on the sofa with a newspaper but he's put that down and has come to sit next to me. His skin is still kind of grey and saggy, but not as grey as it was on the day I saw him collapse at the manor.

'So you saw her,' he says. 'I did too. That day I had my heart attack, of course. But once before that, a few years ago. I've never forgotten it.'

I can't speak for a moment. I've got a mixture of confusing feelings. I'm so relieved that somebody else understands and that I'm not the only one other than Sid who has had things happen to them at Weston Manor. But I'm scared too. Scared that what I saw must be real, or at least real enough for somebody as normal and alive as Sid to know all about it.

'What happened?' I say. I really don't want to hear his answer. But I NEED to know. I need to know I'm not the only crazy person in the manor. Or maybe if Sid has seen something similar to me, I'm not actually crazy at all.

He gets up and puts his shoes on.

'Let's go outside and sit in the sunshine,' he says. 'Remind ourselves that there's life and birds and summer going on outside. This isn't a pretty story. Might as well have a pretty backdrop.'

I nod and follow him outside with Ben holding my hand as usual. He's stopped shaking now but he's very subdued. Not surprising, given the fact that both of us have just escaped abduction by a member of the undead in a black dress.

Mrs Sid brings out another tray of tea and a large chocolate cake and puts them in front of us. Then she places her hand on Sid's shoulder for a brief moment, gives me a smile and vanishes back inside again to do some washing up.

'I like your garden,' I say.

It's true – I do. It's not huge, but divided up into sections with a pond in one, some decking in another and a rockery studded with tiny flowers in yet another. Birds hang and chatter from nut feeders and bird tables.

I think of the enormous grounds at Weston Manor with the kitchen garden and old stables and remains of greenhouses and the tiny pet cemetery which I haven't really explored and I feel dizzy for a moment, so I look around Sid's neat garden again and feel better.

My heart has stopped pounding quite so

hard now and I just feel really tired and limp, like all my blood has turned to heavy lead or something.

I eat some of Mrs Sid's gorgeous cake and feel a bit of life coming back into my body.

'So tell me what you saw,' I say.

Sid settles back in his chair and gazes off into the sky over my right shoulder for a moment.

'It's OK,' I tell him, 'I've seen the scariest things I've ever seen over the past few weeks. I don't think that I could really be much more scared.'

Sid nods and slurps from his cup.

'I was going upstairs one morning to unlock Lady Thomas-Fulford's bedroom,' he says. 'Done it every day for fifteen years. Didn't think much of it. But when I started to climb the stairs it went ice-cold, like. Freezing, it was.'

I clutch Ben. I can feel myself getting cold just listening.

'I carried on up,' he says. 'Just as I got to the top a woman came out of the library, crossed the landing and went straight through the door of Lady Thomas-Fulford's bedroom.'

'Through?' I say. 'Like – through the wood?'

'That's it,' says Sid. 'Exactly. She were wearing a long black dress with a kind of bustle thing on the back. She didn't look at me and I didn't see her face, thank the Lord. Just disappeared into that bedroom.'

I feel sick now. I can see what he's describing as clearly as if it had happened to me.

'What did you do then?' I say. I have visions of Sid bolting downstairs and running out of the entrance hall at Weston Manor and straight down the outside steps and off down the drive, never to be seen again. And yet – he was still working there when my family moved in.

'I went upstairs and I unlocked that bedroom door,' says Sid.

I shoot him a look of horror.

'But how could you?' I stammer. 'I mean – she might have been in there.'

'She might, but she wasn't,' says Sid. 'It's my job to unlock those bedrooms, so unlock them I did.'

I gaze at Sid with a new respect.

'No way would I have done that,' I whisper.

'Well, when I came back downstairs I was dead pale, like,' says Sid. 'Dawn asked me if I'd seen a ghost!'

I give a shaky laugh. Then I tell Sid about everything that's happened to me at the manor. I tell him about the ladies I saw playing croquet and the ladies chatting by the fireplace and in the graveyard and the day I saw the house with the fire blazing in the grate and the woman in the dining room sobbing and the heavy footsteps on the stairs and the sounds of bells ringing and the weird smells in the morning room and even in my own bedroom. Then I take a deep breath and tell him what happened to me and Ben today in the walled garden.

He listens without speaking, looking me straight in the eye, only moving a hand to bring his cup to his lips from time to time.

Mrs Sid creeps out while I'm talking and puts a couple of tiny tablets on his plate. He gulps them down without his eyes ever leaving my face.

When I've finished I feel tired but better. It's good to get it all out at last.

'Funny place, old Weston,' says Sid. 'Did you know that my mother used to work there? Many years ago. She was one of Lady Thomas-Fulford's servants. After Lady Thomas-Fulford died, she carried on working there. I used to play on the servants' staircase as a little boy in those days. One day I was walking down the stairs when I heard footsteps right behind me, coming down the same way. Strong smell of perfume. I turned round but there was nobody there. Another time I was playing on my little bike in the main entrance hall and I remember going ice-cold and something pushing me on the bike. I never saw what it was.'

I shiver again, a great big shudder that is so violent that Ben nearly falls off my lap.

'What did you do?' I say.

'Ran home and didn't go back inside the place for over forty years,' he says. 'But then the security job came up and I've always had a fondness for the place. Yes, really,' he adds, seeing my astonished face. 'It's a one-off, Weston. You won't find anywhere like it.'

'Thank God,' I mutter. Sid smiles and shakes his head at me.

'Eleanor Thomas-Fulford was devoted to the manor,' he continues, pouring me more tea. 'She didn't want to die and leave it. And her only son was a huge disappointment, so she didn't want him to inherit the house either. That's why she left it to the council instead. He was furious, as you might imagine. Some people say that he's still hanging around the manor too, see. He plays tricks – shouts, turns lights off, that sort of thing.'

I remember the tug on my jeans and the shouting and the cough in my ear and my hand trembles on the cup and saucer.

'Her ladyship had a lot of servants too,' says Sid. 'She treated them very harshly. Made them wear blue serge uniforms, which was most unusual in those days. Most of the servants in the big houses wore black and white.'

I sit up straight, my eyes bulging.

'I saw one of them!' I say. 'I saw one of the servants!'

'Aye. You probably saw Mary-Anne Green,' he says. 'Captain Jack got her pregnant and then refused to support her. Lady Eleanor paid her just enough money to buy her silence. They couldn't have lived with the disgrace, you see. They were a grand society family.'

I think of the woman sobbing in the corner of my bedroom and for a moment I feel sorry for her, before remembering that actually she's supposed to have been DEAD for years and years. I shudder again.

Then I remember something. 'Why do I keep smelling lavender?' I say.

Sid smiles, although his smile is weary, like he doesn't really want to drag up all this stuff.

'That'll be Lady Eleanor,' he says. 'She loved lavender. The house was always full of it. You'll have seen that it still grows all over the garden.'

I nod and chew my lip. Ben is getting fractious and wriggling about too hard. He probably wants to go home.

If we even still *have* a home.

'She's not happy,' Sid is saying. 'Lady Eleanor. She's not happy to have died and left Weston. She's been known to pop up on the anniversary of her death.'

As soon as Sid says that I remember the date on her gravestone.

'It's today, isn't it?' I say. 'Twenty-sixth of June.'

'Aye,' Sid replies. His face looks old in the harsh sunlight. Then it lights up.

'Her half-sisters were great fun, though,' he says. 'Lucinda and Rose. The twins. I remember them coming back to the manor as old ladies. Delightful, they were. I went to both their funerals in the 1950s. They tend to pop up at the manor just before Lady Eleanor makes an appearance.'

'I saw them,' I whisper.

'Aye, pet,' says Sid. 'I know you did. I was there that day in the hall, remember? Dawn saw them as well, but she didn't want to frighten you.'

He leans back and sighs. Mrs Sid comes out with more tea for me and a glass of something for her husband.

'I know it's a bit early for a drink,' she says. 'And the doctors have said you're not to have too much of it. But I reckon you could do with a drop.' Sid reaches up and squeezes her arm.

I wait as he downs the drink in one. He makes a smacking noise with his lips and then places both hands on the table with his arms stretched out straight. He looks me right in the eye. I clutch on to Ben because I feel dizzy.

'So she doesn't appear all the time?' I say.

'Lady Eleanor.'

'No, lass,' he says. 'Things have been quiet for a while. Not so many sightings of her over the last few years.'

'But – I keep seeing her,' I say.

Sid rubs his eyes and leans back in his chair.

'Some people have a sort of gift, I suppose,' he says. 'You've heard of the Stone Tape Theory?'

I look puzzled so he sighs and tops up my tea.

'It's when spirits kind of get recorded into the walls of houses where they've lived,' he says. 'And if there have been strong emotions involved, it only takes a sensitive soul with a particular gift to step into the building and catch past events just sort of replaying themselves as they've done for hundreds of years. You'll probably find that somebody else in your family has that same sensitivity, pet.'

'Yeah,' I say. 'My gran. She's always seeing things that aren't there.'

'Or maybe,' says Sid, 'maybe they are.'

I sit silent for a moment, digesting all this.

'Of course,' he says. 'If your gran has the gift, it's quite likely that your mum does too.'

Mum! But she never seems to see or hear *anything*. And she never really talks about what's been happening to me at the manor.

Ben has given up wriggling and fallen asleep with his thumb in his mouth.

'So maybe I'm sensitive, like my gran,' I say. 'OK. I get that. But it's like Lady Eleanor wants something from me! Why has she come after me, and what does she want? I don't understand! And why do I see her, when Mum and Dad don't?'

When Sid looks at me this time his eyes are full of pain and sadness and something else.

Pity.

Yes, that's it. He looks sorry for me.

'We'll talk more tomorrow,' he says. 'I reckon that's enough for you to deal with today.'

Chapter Sixteen

I stay the night with Sid and Mrs Sid because
I just don't want to go home.

There are things I've got to face. But I don't
want to face them.

Not yet.

Mrs Sid is really nice and she makes me a
huge cooked breakfast and then a faint colour
comes back into my cheeks at last. Jake texts
me and Mrs Sid invites him to come round to
visit and we have a good time playing board
games and chatting, but all the time there's
like this undercurrent of tension and Jake
gives me these sideways, shifty looks like he's

trying to work out who I am. Sometimes I catch Sid looking at me with that strange expression again and my stomach shifts and churns, and for a moment I feel cut loose, like all my roots have been snipped with big scissors and I've been left naked and adrift in a big sea of dark stuff.

After Jake goes, Ben and I are sitting out in the colourful little garden and sharing a glass of coke when Sid comes out, looking all serious.

'There's something else,' he says. 'Something I should tell you, so that it all makes more sense.'

My insides contract. I kind of don't want to know any more about the manor. I don't think I can take it, but Sid's been so kind that I nod and try to look open and interested.

'The little baby I mentioned,' he says.

'The one born to the servant girl. Lady Eleanor adopted him,' he says. 'She adored him. Treated him as her own son.'

'Oh,' I say. 'That's kind.' I'm wondering why Sid looks so worried.

'He died,' says Sid. 'Little Albert. Got rheumatic fever and died just after his fifth birthday.'

I've gone cold from head to foot.

'The grave,' I manage through dry lips. 'I saw the grave.'

Sid looks at me. 'Lady Eleanor never got over it,' he says. 'Ever since then she roams about the manor, although we'd seen hardly anything until your family moved in. Some say she's looking for her lost child.'

The hair on my arms stands to attention. I put my fork down on the plate of uneaten cake in front of me. For one second I feel that buzz in my ears again and smell the rosemary and lavender from the manor walled garden.

'But why's she after me, then?' I say. 'I don't understand.'

And it's true – at that moment, my head is muddled and nothing makes sense.

Sid leans fowards and rests his elbows on his knees so that he can gaze straight into my eyes. 'Now, Tabs,' he says. 'You know why, lass. Yes. You know.'

And I shiver, but after a moment I get it and I nod.

The next day Dad turns up at the door to take me home.

There's somebody else standing right behind him. Somebody smiling at me with her arms held out.

'Mum!'

She folds her arms around me and buries her chin in the top of my head. It feels so good that I never want to let go. Ben joins in the hug and we stand there on Sid's doorstep hugging in a little world of our own while Dad hovers all awkward to one side, making apologetic grimaces.

Sid gives Dad one of his wise looks, but says nothing.

We've already agreed that there's not much point me telling my parents about everything I've experienced at the manor.

'People that don't believe will just tell you you're mad,' says Sid. 'Trust me, I know! That's why over the years I've kept quiet about it. But you know it well now, lass, don't you?'

We exchange smiles.

'Are you sure I can't persuade you to come back to work?' Dad is asking Sid.

Sid catches my eye.

'You know,' he says, 'I've been meaning to take early retirement and treat my missus to one or two of them foreign holidays that everybody takes. So – no. I don't think I will.'

Dad nods, even though he looks sad. I feel sad too. I'm going to miss seeing Sid.

And now Mum and Dad are bundling me into the car to take me home and they are thanking Sid and Mrs Sid. She's kissing me and she holds my hand firmly, just for a fraction longer than necessary, and our eyes meet as I sit in the back of the car and I get a lump in my throat because Sid and his wife have helped me feel sane again.

Well – almost.

We drive back to the manor and Mum and Dad make a real effort to talk to one another in kind voices and I know it's all for my sake, so I smile and try to chat about school and Jake and normal things even though it's hard. When I see the squareness of the manor loom up in front of us a shadow falls across my heart but I keep the smiling up so that they don't notice.

'Are you home for good, Mum?' I say as we enter the flat.

Mum strokes my hair out of my face. 'I'm home for you at the moment,' she says. 'That's what matters. Me and Dad will sort out the other stuff later.'

Dad flushes when she says this but he goes out for takeaway and we try to have a normal family evening in front of the television, and all the time I'm aware of the manor just sitting there outside our door and waiting for me to do goodness knows what. I wonder if maybe the talk with Sid has somehow exorcised the spirits and that they might get bored with trying to frighten me now.

Then Ben starts playing up and kicking my legs so I pull a face and shout, 'OW!' and then he does it again, only harder and this time I feel teeth biting at my foot, so I yell even louder and try to toss him off my leg. But he carries on messing about so I have to keep shouting even though Mum and Dad are trying to watch television and in the end I just really lose my temper and I shout, 'Ben! Will you STOP that, please?' And then I realise that the television has gone quiet because Mum has switched it off at the remote and, even though Ben has stopped biting me, I'm aware that the sofa is kind of wobbling under where I'm sitting – and then I see.

It's Mum.

She's crying.

Great silent shaking sobs into her hands. They're pressed right over her face and her shoulders are going up and down.

'Oh, for Christ's sake,' says Dad. 'Well done, Tabitha. We've been back five minutes. And now this.'

'It's not my fault if Ben's biting me!' I say.

Mum cries harder but she's looking up at Dad through wet eyes full of hatred.

'Don't you DARE blame Tabitha for everything!' she says. 'We're hardly in a position to blame HER, are we?'

Dad makes a groaning noise and goes over to stand by the window. Mum's crying so hard now that I'm frightened. Ben gets off my leg and goes to hide under the kitchen table.

When Dad turns round he looks furious. He glares at me and I sink against Mum for comfort.

I know what's coming.

Nobody's dared say it to me for well over a year. They've been hoping I'll grow out of it, I suppose.

But I haven't.

'Tabitha,' says Dad. He looks more like himself again now, less angry and just tired.

He comes over and crouches at my feet in a

most un-Dad-like way. I'm not used to him being smaller than me.

He takes my hands in his big warm ones and then he says it.

'This has got to stop.'

Chapter Seventeen

I t's a hot summer's day just one year ago and
I'm playing out in the Pavilion Gardens
with Ben.

The Pavilion is right in the centre of town.
It's always looked quite weird having such a
grand palace surrounded by parks and shops
and traffic and normal life. The carved gothic
towers stretch up over the surrounding
buildings so that wherever you are, you can
always see how to get back there.

We have a private bit of garden because
Dad's the Keeper so it comes with our large
flat. There's a gate, which leads out of the

walled garden and on to the main road, but Mum and Dad always keep it locked to stop the public from snooping around and trying to peer into our home.

It's worked, or at least, up until now.

I'm supposed to be looking after Ben.

'You're thirteen now,' Mum says. 'Old enough to have some responsibility.'

Mum loves living at the Pavilion. Sometimes she sneaks out of our flat at night and goes downstairs to the Great Ballroom to dance. I followed her once and watched her twirl and stretch around the red carpet under the high domed roof.

I don't love the house so much.

My mates reckon it's the coolest thing ever when they come over after school and I show them around a palace with Dad's bunch of keys jangling like skeleton bones on my hip, but I've kind of got used to it now.

Sometimes it stinks.

I told Mum once after a really bad night when I hadn't had any sleep and she sighed.

'Big houses have very old and complicated plumbing systems, Tabs,' she said. 'It can sound a lot like other things. But it's just pipes and water.'

Pipes and water.

Er, right.

Sometimes I think Mum must see me as a bit of an idiot or something.

I mean – there's no way that what I hear in the night is 'pipes and water'.

So on this hot summers day, Mum and Dad go off to the Palace Theatre down the road and they leave me in charge of my four-year-old brother and we play on the swings that Dad has put up for us and we eat a picnic supper of scotch eggs and ham sandwiches. Ben goes to sleep on the picnic rug so I wander into the flat and get some ice cream out of the freezer and then decide that I want the chocolate sauce that hardens into a crispy shell, so I hunt through all Mum's cupboards and when I go back outside with a bowl for myself and another for Ben I see that the rug is empty.

I don't panic.

Not at first.

Ben is always off hiding and then springing out to surprise you, so I look behind all the big trees and shout, 'Coming, ready or not!' And then after a while it does seem very quiet in the walled garden so I go into the flat and look around just in case he's slipped back in and then my heart starts to thud a bit harder and another five minutes pass so I start to yell his name out quite loud around the garden and there's no reply.

I ring Mum's mobile but it's switched off for the theatre.

She said that if there was an emergency I should call the Pavilion security guard, so I ring his number and he turns up a few minutes later in his dark uniform and hunts about with me a bit. Then says he reckons he should ring the police and that's when I notice that the gate in the brick wall is open. I run out on to the main road in a panic and start shouting Ben's name really loudly and there's loads of cars jammed up in a queue outside and groups of people standing about in the middle of the road and when I go back into the garden and into the flat, the security guard is standing in our lounge talking to a load of other people in uniform. At first, I think they're his friends from the Pavilion and then I realise that they're all looking at me in a particular way and that they're actually policemen. After that my head goes dark and swimmy and somebody tells me to put it between my legs. Then Mum and Dad are back and Mum is screaming, 'NO! NO! NO!' over and over and Dad is trying to comfort her and neither of them look at me.

They don't look at me for days after that.

It was my fault, you see. Somebody else might have left the gate unlocked but I was supposed to be looking after Ben.

And I didn't.

Which is why he came back to haunt me and . . .

I've been looking after him ever since.

Chapter Eighteen

Mum, Dad and I leave Weston Manor two weeks later.

We have to.

I've had two sessions with a new counsellor. I have to talk about Ben and my feelings about his death and so far it seems to be going kind of OK.

But Dad says we need to start a new life and that he can't be a Keeper in a grand house any longer. He's going to look for a day job at a museum and we're to live with Gran until he can afford to buy us a new house of our own. I'm going to stay at the same school though, which is kind of cool. I've had a chat with Jake and tried to convince him that I'm not raving mad and I think he understands. We're going to meet up in few weeks, although I don't know if he will turn up and, in a way, I'd understand if he didn't. I hope he does, but he's seen all my weirdness now and let's face it, Tabitha Grey is never going to be 'normal'.

'We need to put you first,' Dad says to me. 'Get you sorted out.'

Thing have changed at the manor anyway.

Dawn has left.

Dad never mentions her. Neither does Mum. It's like it never happened, except that Mum and Dad are also going to counselling now to try to save their marriage.

We move out of Weston on a rainy July day.

Dad's car is pulled up outside ready. For a moment the four of us stand in a line looking up at the manor.

It looks back from its dark green shuttered eyes and white face.

Mum's hair blows around her face. She's struggling not to cry.

Dad stares at the manor and I can tell he's missing his job as Keeper already.

I look up at the building and I don't feel an awful lot. Not any more.

Empty, on the whole.

I've used up all my emotion. Nosebleeds have stopped too.

There's a tug on my hand.

Ben.

He looks fainter now, less real. I can see through his stomach to the grass on the front lawn behind. I look down at his dark head and I let go of his hand.

'Go on,' I say. 'I can't look after you any more.'

I push him in the direction of the manor.

He takes a few trembling steps away from us. His family.

I get into the car quick. Mum and Dad are already in and Dad starts up the engine.

'Bye, Weston,' Dad says. He puts the car into gear and we start to move.

'Bye,' I echo.

Ben stands on the top step staring after us. He looks so small and alone that my heart contracts.

'Look at him,' Mum whispers. 'He never smiles any more.'

I grip her shoulder.

'You mean,' I start. 'You mean – you can *see* him?'

Mum nods. There are tears running down her cheeks.

'Always have, Tabs,' she says. 'And it was my fault as much as yours. You see – it was me who forgot to lock that gate.'

The car swings out of the drive, crunching over the gravel.

I don't want to, but something makes me turn round for a last look.

Ben's still standing by the big entrance door to the manor.

He's not alone.

There's a woman wearing a long black dress. She takes his hand.

They go inside and shut the door.

Acknowledgements

Weston Manor is based on Preston Manor in Brighton, Sussex. I'd like to thank the staff for their help in promoting and researching this book, in particular Paula Wrightson whose tremendous enthusiasm for the project has shone throughout. Thanks also to Margaret Muskett for introducing me to Preston Manor in the first place, to Tim Brown of the Paranormal Investigation Group Sussex for his early advice when I was researching the book, to Imelda Joanne Thomas for sharing my love of all things unexplained and to Leah, Philippa and the team at Egmont for all their hard work and encouragement.

EGMONT PRESS: ETHICAL PUBLISHING

Egmont Press is about turning writers into successful authors and children into passionate readers – producing books that enrich and entertain. As a responsible children's publisher, we go even further, considering the world in which our consumers are growing up.

Safety First
Naturally, all of our books meet legal safety requirements. But we go further than this; every book with play value is tested to the highest standards – if it fails, it's back to the drawing-board.

Made Fairly
We are working to ensure that the workers involved in our supply chain – the people that make our books – are treated with fairness and respect.

Responsible Forestry
We are committed to ensuring all our papers come from environmentally and socially responsible forest sources.

For more information, please visit our website at www.egmont.co.uk/ethical